BEAUTIFULLY GUARDED

CANDIED CRUSH #17

CHARITY PARKERSON

Punk
&
Sissy

—Warning: This book is intended for readers over the age of 18.

Copyright © 2021 Charity Parkerson
Editor: BZ Hercules & Editing
Photographer: Period Images
ISBN: 978-1-946099-89-1
All rights reserved.

❀ Created with Vellum

INTRODUCTION

COOPER IS MORE THAN HE SEEMS. TITO HAS KNOWN IT ALL ALONG. NOW IT'S TIME TO FACE THE MUSIC.

After two years of homelessness, Cooper has settled into living with his chosen family. He loves his new lease on life. There's just one problem. His old life is coming to reclaim him, and Cooper isn't strong enough to face the past alone. Thankfully, there's a sexy bodyguard who never leaves Cooper's side.

Since Cooper came to live with Tito's boss, Tito has been fascinated by Cooper's many layers. He's known all along Cooper has secrets. Tito just wasn't expecting them to be so big. That doesn't mean he intends to let Cooper face anything alone, because Tito is hiding something too. He's completely in love with Cooper.

When two worlds collide, both men will have to

find their footing. Only time will tell if their relationship will still be standing at the end.

ONE

THE TURQUOISE WATERS in Ibiza mesmerized Cooper. He wanted to sit and stare all day. His life had been such a series of ups and downs over the past few years. After spending two years homeless, he had ended up here, sitting in one of the most beautiful places he had ever been. That last bit was all thanks to Rocky. Cooper had won the lottery when Rocky had taken him in. At first, Cooper had been meant to work as a security guard for some billionaire under Rocky. Then Rocky had moved in with his men, Hudson and Jinx, taking Cooper with him. Now, he was on the throuple's honeymoon with them. Life was surreal as fuck sometimes. Cooper could have never seen this coming two years ago when he had spent his first night sleeping in the street. Yet he couldn't imagine being anywhere else. He loved the throuple who had essentially adopted him.

A man in the distance caught Cooper's eye. He was huge and covered in tattoos. When Cooper had met Tito, Tito had kept his head shaved bald, making him look twice as menacing. Now Tito was slowly growing his dark hair back. It was at that stage where it was always a mess. Tito was a bit terrifying. He looked mean. Cooper imagined that was part of his job as Hudson's personal bodyguard. Since Cooper was only five-five and skinny as hell, Tito could likely crush Cooper beneath his heel. Yet he still made Cooper's heart race every time they were together. In swim trunks and nothing else, Tito had other parts of Cooper's body stirring as well as he came to stand over Cooper's beach chair.

Tito dropped his surfboard next to Cooper in the sand. "You're starting to burn." Tito went down onto his knees beside Cooper. "Did you put on sunscreen?"

. . .

With the light hitting Tito's hazel eyes, Cooper had a hard time holding on to the threads of their conversation. "Um. Yeah. I put some on before coming out."

"That was hours ago." Tito dug through their beach bag and came out with the sunscreen. He popped the lid open. "Have you at least been staying hydrated?"

A laugh burst from Cooper. "Yes, Mother. I've been drinking my water."

Tito scowled at Cooper's flippant tone.

Cooper's laughter died as Tito slathered sunscreen across his torso. Only God knew how hard Cooper had to fight to keep from embarrassing himself with Tito's hands on his body, massaging sunscreen into Cooper's skin. Cooper tried thinking about something else. "You looked great out there in the water. I've always wanted to learn how to surf, but I wasn't allowed outside very often as a kid."

Tito kept his gaze locked on his task. "I could teach you."

The thought of humiliating himself in front of Tito had Cooper immediately blowing off the suggestion. "It's okay. I'm not a very strong swimmer. As much as I'd like to try it, I'm scared of drowning."

Tito didn't respond right away. He coated Cooper's face with sunscreen. When he finished, he pulled Cooper to his feet. "I have an idea." He grabbed his surfboard and towed Cooper toward the water.

There was a small building near the water's edge stocked with different boards, life jackets, and water toys. Tito stopped to switch to a different board and grab a life jacket. Cooper stood still while Tito dressed him in the life jacket, as if he were a child.

Then he motioned toward the larger board he had exchanged.

"This is a tandem board. This way, you can ride with me."

Cooper tried not to show the way his nerves frayed at the idea. The thought of spending quality time with Tito outweighed everything. "Okay."

At his agreement, Tito led Cooper to the water. Side by side, they moved deeper until they were holding on to the board and swimming against the waves. When they got to a spot where they were in deep enough that they couldn't stand, but the water was still calm, Tito showed Cooper how to sit on the board. Once he was settled, Tito joined him. Cooper's back rested against Tito's huge chest. He felt completely safe in Tito's arms. Small waves bobbed beneath them, rocking them.

. . .

Tito's lips touched the shell of Cooper's ear. "Lean forward. Together, we'll use our arms to paddle alongside the waves, then I'll stand, and you'll move to your knees. You just hang on for now."

Cooper did as instructed. His heart raced as the waves increased in size and the board moved faster. Then Tito stood, Cooper moved to his knees, and the water became like a tunnel. A laugh burst from Cooper's chest as they came out the other side unscathed. Tito settled in behind him again as the water calmed. His arms encircled Cooper's waist. He dragged Cooper back into his embrace. Cooper's spine relaxed. Air filled his lungs. Cooper always felt like he had come home every time he sat in Tito's company. He couldn't explain it. They just felt right. It was like they had known each other their entire lives.

Time passed, and the sun dipped low. It took some coaxing, but Tito got Cooper standing too. They fell a few times and Cooper was exhausted by the time he managed to stay upright, but he enjoyed every second. In fact, it turned out to be the best day of his life. Cooper had lived through hard enough times that he understood he needed to cherish the good days. He would remember this one forever.

"I'm starving. Let's head back to the house and order something to eat."

Cooper didn't want to give up his spot in Tito's arms, but he was pretty damn hungry too. Starving had been the worst part of living in the streets. The first few weeks of living with Rocky, Cooper had stolen tons of food and hidden it in his assigned bedroom. It had taken some time for him to accept he could eat regular meals again without hoarding. Now he hated skipping meals.

"Sounds good."

Together, they made their way back to shore. Cooper gathered his things while Tito returned the board and life jacket. The house they were renting for the month-long honeymoon came fully stocked with everything to enjoy their stay on their private beach. Still, Tito locked the supply building to be safe. Side by side, they rinsed the sand from their feet and legs before heading inside. Cooper dropped the sandy beach bag inside the mudroom.

"We should probably snag a shower before eating."

Cooper nodded at the suggestion. Between spending all day in the sun and the workout of learning to surf, he was drained. Thankfully, each bedroom had a private bathroom. They headed through the kitchen and living room before going upstairs. Tito led the way. They parted ways as they reached their bedrooms, which were next door to each other. Cooper noticed the honeymooners still hadn't left their bedroom down the hall. He wondered if they had ventured out all day. Not that Cooper was complaining. He liked having Tito to himself. If Hudson decided to go somewhere, Tito would have to go too. Thankfully, so far, Hudson had let Tito treat this trip like a vacation. They didn't go out often. When they did, it was usually on a planned outing for fun adventures. It had been a great trip.

The sensation of Tito holding him while they bobbed on the waves swept through Cooper's mind as he stepped inside the shower. Cooper kind of hoped this trip never ended.

Every muscle Tito had felt stiff from restraining himself all day. Since a tiny five-foot-five blond angel walked into his life, Tito had been a mess. Each time he stared into Cooper's light green eyes, he lost another piece of himself. Tito was a bodyguard. That was who he had been for years. He had gotten the gig of being Hudson Vincent's personal guard at eighteen. Tito had seen it as the blessing it was and never taken the role for granted. Being a protector was in his blood. So, when a tiny, malnourished Cooper had shown up in his life, Tito had been drawn to him. Every overprotective cell in his body had gravitated to sheltering Cooper. Now Tito wanted to keep him.

The hot water felt too good on Tito's sore muscles. He lingered longer than necessary. Tito was hyper aware of Cooper showering in the next room. Only a thin wall separated him from paradise. He forced himself to stay on task. Cooper deserved better than to have Tito fantasizing about having Cooper's body beneath him. They were only friends. Tito had to remind himself of that for the millionth time. Cooper had no clue how Tito felt. Things needed to stay that way. Tito was almost eleven years older than Cooper. Cooper was super young. Tito needed to stop wishing the wall between them would disappear. Tito ruthlessly turned off the hot water and finished his shower with only ice-cold water raining down on him. It was what he deserved.

By the time Tito dressed and left his room, Cooper's bedroom door stood open. Tito peeked inside, finding the room empty. He headed downstairs. Cooper was face down on the couch, asleep. A smile tugged at the corners of Tito's mouth at the sight. Tito swore the guy could sleep anywhere. His smile fell as he recalled why. Cooper had spent countless nights sleeping in alleyways and ditches, cold and dirty. Tito grabbed a blanket and covered Cooper's body. Unfortunately, Hudson, Jinx, and Rocky chose that moment to finally emerge from their bedroom. The three men were like the Three Bears: small, medium, and large. The only thing remotely similar about them was their brown hair. Otherwise, the throuple couldn't be less alike.

Tito rushed to intercept them before they woke Cooper. He met them at the bottom of the stairs. "Hey, guys. Are you going out?"

Hudson nodded. His nose ring captured the light from the chandelier above the stairs and twinkled. "Yeah. There's a restaurant nearby we want to try."

Tito cast a quick glance Cooper's way before pasting on a fake smile. "Okay. I'll get dressed."

Jinx followed Tito's gaze. "Oh, no. Cooper is asleep." His voice sounded fake as hell, confusing Tito. Then he wrapped his arm around Hudson and started back up the stairs, clearing up the matter. "Maybe we should just go back to bed."

. . .

Rocky cut off their path. "Babe, I'm hungry. Just wake his ass up. He needs to eat too."

Hudson flashed his men a heated glance. "I'm good to go back to bed."

Tito saw his chance. "How about this? Tell me the name of the restaurant, you three go back to bed, and I'll get us takeout from there. I'll even deliver it to your room when I get back."

The three men exchanged glances. Rocky gave in. "I mean, I could go back to bed."

Hudson herded everyone back up the stairs. "Let's go figure out what we want so Tito can get it."

As a unit, they headed up. Tito cast another quick look Cooper's way. He was still asleep. Tito would grab him some food anyhow. That way, Cooper wouldn't go hungry when he woke. He rushed through writing down the guys' orders. When he called to place the takeout order, Tito discovered he could have the food delivered. His relief was palpable. Tito was tired, and he kind of wanted to watch Cooper sleep for a little while.

Cooper was an enigma. According to Jinx, Cooper's mom had put him out at sixteen after learning he was gay. Cooper rarely said anything about his past. His earlier confession about not getting to play outside was the first thing Tito could recall Cooper saying about his childhood at all. Oddly, Cooper was more open about his time on the streets. Tito assumed talking about his family was painful for Cooper, so Tito never pushed.

After their food arrived and Tito delivered to his bosses upstairs, as promised, Tito sat on the living room floor and ate. He waited for the smell of food to wake Cooper. It didn't. Cooper slept soundly while Tito watched. He looked like an angel when awake. Sleeping, Cooper looked innocent as hell... and young. He made Tito feel like a lecher. Honestly, though, Tito just wanted to keep him safe. It didn't take much inspection of Cooper's features and body to see he had been abused at some point. His small frame spoke of years of malnutrition and there was a slight bump on his nose where it had obviously been broken at some point. Then there were the light scars across Cooper's back. Tito hadn't seen those before they arrived here and took their first beach trip. Even then, Cooper visibly took great pains to keep his bare back turned away from people. When Tito had put him in a life jacket, Cooper had visibly fought to keep his back hidden until after the life jacket was on. Then he had relaxed. Tito didn't think Cooper was even conscious of the act anymore. He kept himself hidden out of habit. Tito needed Cooper to know he was safe now. He would always be protected as long as there was breath left in Tito's body to guard him. Tito loved him.

He hadn't quite decided yet what type of love he felt. Tito had never been in love before. Obviously, he loved his parents and siblings. This wasn't the same. He felt good in Cooper's company, and wanted. There was a ton of heat between them, but not in a rushed way. There was no desperation to rip the clothes from Cooper and fuck him fast and hard.

Tito wanted to wait until Cooper came to him. He needed Cooper to be ready for Tito's love. Tito wasn't going anywhere.

With his food gone, it became obvious Cooper needed sleep more than food. Tito stood and picked up his mess. After stashing Cooper's food in the fridge, Tito returned to Cooper's side. He couldn't leave Cooper downstairs unguarded all night. Tito gently rolled Cooper before lifting him into his arms. Cooper's eyes opened for half a second before closing again. Tito moved slowly, trying not to wake Cooper as he carried him up the stairs. It took a little doing for Tito to get him tucked into bed. As he adjusted Cooper's pillow, Cooper's arms encircled Tito's neck. He pulled Tito in for a hug. Even though he didn't have Tito in a tight hold, Tito was still helpless to move away.

Cooper's lips touched the shell of Tito's ear in the lightest of kisses. "Goodnight."

.   .   .

Tito drew a slow and steadying breath. His body was on fire from one small kiss. "Goodnight, angel."

Cooper rolled away and snuggled deeper beneath the blankets. Tito stared down at him with his heart in his throat. One day, they would be more. Tito felt that in his soul.

TWO

MID-MORNING, Cooper woke up well rested, starving, and completely alone in the house. He reheated a container of food from the fridge with his name on it while wondering where everyone had gone. After eating, he searched the large beach house once more before giving up and changing into his swim trunks. Cooper grabbed the beach bag and headed back out to where he started his day yesterday.

The sounds of seagulls and waves soothed him as the scent of seaweed filled his nose. Heat baked his skin while Cooper lost himself in a book of mystery and horror. Hours passed without his notice as he turned the pages. He only stopped reading to get fresh drinks and readjust his umbrella, keeping the sun from frying him alive. The day was nearly gone before a shadow blocked the last of his dying light.

Cooper glanced up.

Tito's huge frame hovered over him. A scowl tugged at his features.

Cooper's eyebrows lifted. "Hey. What's wrong?"

"You didn't call."

Confusion had Cooper setting his book aside. "Was I supposed to?"

Tito nodded. "I left a note by your bed to call me when you were up and moving. That way I could pick you up and you could spend the day touring the city with the guys. I've been calling all day and you haven't answered."

"Oh." Cooper moved his feet so Tito could sit down. "My phone is still plugged in upstairs. I didn't see your note." He also hadn't looked for one.

Tito ignored the fact that Cooper had made room for him to sit. Instead, he continued hovering, making Cooper nervous. "Why did Rocky buy you a phone if you're not going to keep it on you?"

Cooper licked his lips nervously. He didn't like the way he felt—like Tito was angry and Cooper was at a disadvantage. "I don't have anyone to call, so I'm not in the habit of carrying it."

"You have me to call."

Something inside Cooper broke. Tito still towered above him, and Cooper's nerves took a dive. "Will you please sit?" Even Cooper heard the slight hysteria in his voice.

Tito's expression cleared. He quickly sat and took Cooper's hand. "Are you okay?"

Even though Cooper's heart raced and there was a roar inside his ears, Cooper tried sounding calm. "Yes. Sorry." Damn. He was a little messed up. He stroked Tito's hand, which held his. "Really. I'm sorry. I got a little nervous with you standing over me while obviously angry with me."

Tito's hand tightened around his. "Stop apologizing. I'm the one who's sorry. I'm not angry. You scared me when you didn't answer the phone. I didn't want to leave you here alone, but Hudson said you looked like you needed the sleep and made me leave you behind."

He was such an overprotective sweetie. Cooper couldn't get enough. "It's fine. I had a peaceful day."

He grabbed the book and showed Tito how much he had read. "See. I'm almost finished with my book."

"Did you eat anything?"

Cooper nodded. "I found the food you left for me in the fridge."

For a moment, Tito stared at Cooper in silence like he lost himself. Finally, he blinked as if coming back to himself. He looked around. "So you had a nice peaceful day. What do you want to do now? Do you want another surfing lesson?"

"Do you ever stop going?" The question was out there before Cooper thought better of it. He tried to explain. "I mean, you're always on the go with Hudson, or working out, or surfing, or running, or doing something with me. What do you do to relax?"

"I'm relaxed right now."

. . .

A laugh burst from Cooper at Tito's response. "This is your down time? Seriously?"

Tito brushed his thumb back and forth across Cooper's. "Yeah. Being with you relaxes me."

Cooper rolled his eyes. He couldn't help it. "Fine. If you're willing to do the tandem thing again, I'll go with you. If you're just trying to entertain me, then don't. Pull a chair closer and sit with me. I don't need to be kept busy."

"I'll change."

Cooper bit his bottom lip as his gaze followed Tito inside. Damn. He really was a beautiful guy. He always dressed in business suits while guarding Hudson, looking the part of a professional. Since Tito was somewhat on vacation, he wore a pair of form-fitting jeans and a t-shirt today. He really, really filled out a pair of jeans. Tito made Cooper's heart race with only one glance. Cooper hadn't known real attraction until he met Tito. He knew Tito looked at him like a little brother. They weren't on the same level, so Cooper got it. Tito was walking perfection. Cooper was the opposite of that. So Cooper was good with being the little brother. He hoped his heart got the memo someday and stopped trying to leap from his chest while he read too much from every touch.

Cooper's gaze dropped to his lap. A long, thin white scar across his upper thigh peeked out from the edge of his shorts. Cooper tugged at the material, hiding the mark. They were too different. Tito could never want someone like him.

"Let's grab a life jacket and board."

Cooper let Tito pull him to his feet. He tried not to stare at Tito's solid chest. As they headed for the water, Cooper made sure he kept pace with Tito so he never got ahead of him. Cooper never let anyone see his back. There was so much about his past he couldn't share. He didn't relax until after a life jacket hid his scars. Some things were too hard to share.

Considering it was only Cooper's second time surfing, he did an amazing job. By the time they were bobbing on the board, sitting face to face straddling the board, Cooper wore a huge smile. His obvious pride had Tito's chest swelling.

"We should keep this up when we get back home. I try to go about once a week."

Cooper shrugged. "Sure. If you don't mind me tagging along, this is fun."

"I like spending time with you." Tito's admission was the tip of the iceberg, but it was a start.

"I like being with you too."

.   .   .

Tito scooted closer. There was a bit of seaweed on Cooper's life jacket. Tito used it as an excuse to touch Cooper and move even closer. After tossing the greenery back into the ocean, Tito dropped his hand to Cooper's knee. A scar on Cooper's thigh drew Tito's touch. He traced the line with his fingertips. Cooper tried tugging his shorts lower to hide the mark from Tito. Tito couldn't take it.

"You know you can tell me anything, right?"

Cooper licked his lips. "Sure." He did not, in fact, sound like he was sure.

"Can I tell you anything too?" Tito asked, trying to lighten the mood.

A smile snapped to Cooper's lips. "Of course."

.   .   .

"Good." Tito enjoyed keeping Cooper slightly off balance. "I don't work out all the time because I have to keep Hudson safe. That's only part of it. I used to be tall and extremely skinny in my early teenage years. People always bullied me. I decided one day I would never be the smallest guy in the room again."

This time, Cooper moved closer. Their knees touched. Cooper's feet toyed with Tito's beneath the water. "I've never been kissed. If I'd ever gone to school, I'm certain that would've been one of a million things I was bullied over."

"You make me want to ask a thousand questions with just one statement."

Cooper's eyes filled with fear. "Please don't."

Tito had to fix things. He couldn't let Cooper be afraid or feel inferior. Tito's heart couldn't take it. "Maybe I should be your first kiss."

. . .

A blush exploded across Cooper's face. He averted his gaze. "You don't have to sacrifice yourself like that. I'm sure you've kissed a thousand guys way better than me while touring with Hudson and have a thousand more guys you'd rather kiss now."

"There's no one I'd rather be with right now."

Cooper's gaze slid back Tito's way at Tito's confession. Tito let some of the desire he felt show in his expression as he slowly leaned Cooper's way. He wanted Cooper to have time to say no. Cooper held his stare. Then desire flared to life in Cooper's eyes before he quickly dropped his gaze to Tito's lips, hiding his feelings. It was too late. Tito knew Cooper wanted him. He closed the final space between them and pressed his lips to Cooper's. It was the lightest of kisses. Tito barely swiped his lips across Cooper's before pulling away a hair. They shared each other's air with only an inch separating them. Triumph rang through Tito when Cooper closed the gap. This time, when their lips met, Tito took things a little farther. His lips parted. Cooper's did too. Tito licked Cooper's bottom lip. Cooper released a stuttered-sounding breath and opened for him. With permission given, Tito's tongue brushed Cooper's. Cooper hesitantly licked him back. Tito held Cooper's face and poured his heart into their kiss. He sucked Cooper's bottom lip before diving back inside his mouth. Their tongues brushed and stroked. Tito's body was on fire, but he kept his hands on Cooper's face. Cooper held on to Tito's thighs.

Even though Tito hadn't gotten anywhere near his fill, he pulled away and pressed his forehead to Cooper's while he tried catching his breath.

"Thank you for being the first."

Cooper had no business thanking him because Tito would be Cooper's last. He had found the one. There was no going back.

Tito's kiss still lingered on Cooper's lips as he showered. He washed the salt and sand from his body on autopilot while his brain relived every second. Cooper couldn't pretend he hadn't fantasized about Tito kissing him. He just hadn't realized how small of an imagination he had. Tito's kiss was soft yet firm. It had been sexy as hell. Kissing Tito felt like what Cooper imagined slow love-making would.

Cooper's eyes slid closed. He recalled every second. The way Tito sucked Cooper's bottom lip wouldn't leave Cooper's mind. That moment played on repeat inside Cooper's head, making Cooper's body burn. Cooper's hand slid down his body and stroked his cock. He immediately pulled away. No. He wouldn't do that. Cooper's eyes burned. He turned off the water and dried his skin, trying not to cry while ignoring his erection. Cooper wanted to scream and scream at the ghosts that wouldn't leave his head. He just wanted to be normal. Why couldn't he stop remembering the past? Cooper just wanted... Tito. Cooper buried his face in the towel and screamed at the top of his lungs. He wanted to rebel against the nightmares that lived in his head, but the fear still lived there too. Cooper couldn't make it stop. He didn't know how.

After getting dry, Cooper found a pair of thin workout shorts and pulled them on. He didn't bother with underwear. Everything felt like too much. Cooper climbed into bed and rolled onto his side. He stared at the wall, trying to make his mind blank. Until he didn't feel this way anymore, Cooper couldn't go back downstairs. He needed to calm down. Jinx, Hudson, Rocky, and Tito were like a real family to him. Cooper didn't want to risk snapping or showing them an ugly side of him. He had to know his limits. Tonight, he was spiraling.

Time passed without Cooper while he ranted inside his head. He berated himself and tried shutting out the voices that did the same. The bed dipped beside him. The scent of Tito's cologne washed over Cooper before Tito's arm draped across him, towing Cooper back against his chest. Cooper's eyes slipped closed as Tito's lips brushed the shell of his ear. "Are you avoiding me?"

. . .

Cooper's eyes shot open. "What? Of course not."

"You missed dinner again."

Cooper deflated. Sometimes Cooper lost himself. "I'm sorry."

Tito ran his hand across Cooper's stomach. "Don't apologize. Just talk to me. I don't like you skipping meals. I'd rather have food delivered directly to your bedroom so you don't have to see me than you not eat."

Cooper rolled onto his back so he could meet Tito's stare. "I'm not avoiding you. Promise. I just lost track of time."

With his head propped up on his hand and his elbow buried in the mattress next to Cooper's head, Tito stared down at him. Up close, Tito's eyelashes looked unnaturally long. His hazel eyes were beautiful.

Cooper forgot all about the bad. Only Tito existed in that moment. His intensity had Cooper taking a steadying breath.

"What are you thinking?" Cooper had to know what thoughts hid behind Tito's heated expression.

Tito didn't let him down. He never did. "I'm wondering if you'll let me kiss you again, and—if you do—how long it'll be before you hate me for it?"

Cooper blinked. "I could never hate you." Cooper fingered the neck of Tito's t-shirt, twisting it until he could draw Tito closer. Tito couldn't know how much bravery it took for Cooper to make the first move. This time, when their lips met, there was no slow build. Cooper was ready for the way Tito dove in, licking and sucking. He wasn't prepared for how fast and hot he burned. Cooper's body screamed to be touched. Tito's hand rested on Cooper's bare stomach. Cooper wanted to beg him to move it lower. He hadn't been able to touch himself earlier, but the more heated their kiss became, the more Cooper realized Tito could touch him.

Desperation took hold. Cooper set his hand over Tito's and guided his touch. Tito took the hint and stroked his erection once. Cooper's hips left the bed, following his touch. Then it was over. Cooper whimpered against Tito's lips. Tito rolled and straddled Cooper's body without barely breaking their kiss. The lower half of Tito's body pressed against his. Then Tito lifted, readjusted his erection, and was back. Cooper moaned as the bulge in Tito's pants rubbed against Cooper's cock. Tito moved against him while they kissed. Tension quickly built inside Cooper. He had been denied this sensation for so long. Now it was Tito making him feel this way, and Tito was hard. That was like a double bonus. Cooper never dreamed Tito could be turned on by him. Yet here they were, making love in their clothes.

Cooper didn't want to come inside his shorts, but he was too scared to lose them. He fought against his building orgasm, scared of embarrassment. Fuck, he needed to come. Cooper had little control. Tito smelled good and tasted even better. Even without having kissed anyone else, Cooper realized Tito had skill. He teased Cooper and made him wild. Cooper moved beneath Tito and fought for more. The pressure climbing his shaft couldn't be denied. Cooper moaned around Tito's tongue. Tito rocked faster against Cooper's body. Cooper dug his nails into Tito's skin, trying to hang on. There was no stopping the ecstasy. Hot cum filled the inside of Cooper's shorts. Tito cried out against Cooper's lips, making the cum issue worse. Cooper's body shook from the power of his release. Then the embarrassment hit.

Heat flooded Cooper's cheeks. Tears pricked the backs of his eyes. His nose burned as he fought not to cry. Tito was way out of Cooper's league, and Cooper had come in his shorts like he had just hit puberty. Cooper knew he would be twice as humiliated if he cried, but he was that horrified. He couldn't help the way he felt. Tito moved away and sat back on his heels. His head fell forward as he looked down the line of his body. The front of his pajama pants were soaked.

. . .

A sexy laugh rumbled from Tito's throat. "Fuck. No one has made me come in my clothes in like fifteen years."

Cooper's horror cleared. He wasn't the only one. He stared at Tito, awestruck. Cooper had made him come. Tito De Luca had orgasmed from touching Cooper. Wow. He forgot to be embarrassed.

Tito's sexy hazel stare met Cooper's gaze. "I guess we should get cleaned up. If you're okay with me staying in here tonight, I'd like to hold you a little longer."

Cooper swallowed past the hope that choked him. "I'd like that too."

With a smile, Tito scrambled from the bed and headed for the door. He looked over his shoulder as he went. "I'll go change and be right back." He peeked out the door as if looking to see if the coast was clear. Obviously finding the hall empty, Tito tossed him a wink and a smile before slipping from the room. A happy laugh burst from Cooper the second he was alone. He couldn't stop smiling. Cooper had no idea where this was headed or if this night would ever be repeated, but he was still wowed. This night had been a blessing. Cooper would never forget it.

THREE

COMING HOME from Ibiza was one part depressing and two parts a relief. Tito was ready to sleep in his own bed. Vacations were nice, even though his were always working vacations. Tito's job never felt like work to him, except for a few times before Hudson fell in love with Jinx and Rocky. Hudson was bipolar, and his manic episodes weren't always easy to deal with. But Hudson was like a brother to Tito, and there was nothing Tito wouldn't do for him. This was the perfect job and home for Tito. Now Cooper shared their home too. It was like finding paradise.

. . .

While they still hadn't done more than kiss and heavy make-out sessions, Tito was more invested than ever. Cooper made Tito feel alive and special. The way Cooper looked at him was addictive. Tito had never felt more like a superhero. He wanted to be perfect in Cooper's eyes; the way Cooper was flawless in his.

Unfortunately, coming back home meant being back to his regular duties. Jinx and Rocky had people to see and errands to run. Hudson wanted to join, which meant Brent had to drive and Tito had to keep Hudson safe. It was a boring day. Thankfully, Cooper tagged along. Brent, Cooper, and Tito played poker in the car while the guys visited their friends, Zayn and Spencer. Despite the distraction, Tito was still more than a little grateful when the guys spilled from the house, ready to go home. After passing heated glances on the sly all day, Tito hoped to spend some time alone with Cooper.

As Brent steered the SUV down the long drive of Hudson's estate, Tito spotted a black Cadillac parked out front. Alarm bells rang in his head and years of experience kicked in. He pulled the phone from his belt and called the security booth.

"Why is there an unknown black car on the property?" Tito asked the moment the front guard answered.

"It's an attorney on official business. His name is Baker Cox. He's here for Cooper."

Tito's head whipped toward the backseat. His gaze met Cooper's. Cooper's eyebrows rose, questioning Tito's stare. Tito turned back around in his seat. "Thank you. I'll take care of it."

When the SUV came to a stop, no one got out. It was obvious everyone waited for Tito to give the okay that it was safe. Instead, he turned in his seat and met Cooper's stare again. "Why is there an attorney named Baker Cox here for you?"

·   ·   ·

There was no slow build or myriad of emotions. Cooper went straight to terrified, with no stops along the way. "No."

Everyone looked Cooper's way.

Cooper immediately began to shake. "No," he repeated, sounding like his teeth chattered.

Tito didn't need to know more. "Okay. I'll take care of it." He jumped from the SUV and headed for the door. Tito found a normal-looking brown-haired and well-dressed man waiting on the front steps. He had a briefcase with him.

Baker stood as Tito approached. "Hello. I'm Baker Cox, an attorney for Wilson and Cox law firm. A fellow at the front gate said I should wait here for Cooper Whitaker."

. . .

Tito wasn't warmed by the British accent. Cooper was scared as hell of this guy. Therefore, he had to go. "Cooper doesn't wish to see you."

Baker dropped his gaze to his shoes for a second before meeting Tito's stare again. "I have no doubt that's true, but—unfortunately—his desires change nothing. There's an important legal matter he cannot avoid."

Fuck. A legal matter sounded important. Tito's mind ran through a million scenarios. Cooper might have been arrested while living in the streets and be in some sort of trouble. This might be something Cooper truly couldn't avoid. He motioned for Baker to wait.

"Give me a second." He headed back to the SUV. The guys were all standing outside the vehicle whispering to each other. Cooper was the only one still sitting in the car. The backdoor stood open, giving Tito a clear look at Cooper. Cooper shook like a leaf while staring at nothing. He was so pale, it was as if there was no blood left in his body.

Rocky cut him off before he made it to Cooper. "What the fuck is going on? Who is this lawyer?"

Tito made a helpless gesture. "I don't know. He says he has a legal matter to discuss with Cooper and it can't be avoided." He chewed his bottom lip and stared at Cooper. Tito had never felt more useless. "I don't know what to do." Hudson and Jinx moved closer while Tito tried to decide how to handle this. "I mean, if he's in some sort of legal trouble, he can't avoid this guy. We have to let him speak with Cooper. Better an attorney than the police."

Rocky cursed under his breath.

Hudson stepped in. "That may be so, but I won't let Cooper speak to this guy alone. Look at him. He's terrified. No way in hell are we abandoning him to anyone's mercy."

. . .

"Has he said anything?"

Hudson shook his head at Tito's question. "He just went pale, started shaking, and clammed up." Hudson shot a look toward where Tito left Baker. "You get Cooper. I want you with him while he talks to this attorney. I'll make sure you're allowed to stay."

With a nod, Tito rushed to Cooper's side and Rocky went with Hudson to deal with the lawyer.

Cooper stared at him with dead eyes.

Tito hated himself for forcing the matter. "It's a legal matter. You have to talk to him, but I'm not leaving your side. Do you have any idea what this is about?"

"He's my family's attorney," Cooper said, sounding like glass cut his throat with every word.

. . .

Tito's heart dropped. Cooper's reaction to seeing his family's attorney proved all Tito's fears about the abuse he suspected. Rage hardened his heart. "You have me. I swear nothing will happen to you as long as I'm at your side. Do you trust me to keep you safe?"

Cooper gave a jerky nod.

Tito took his hand. "Okay, then. Let's go. Hang on to me and I'll protect you."

Cooper's knees buckled slightly as he stepped out. Tito had to keep him upright. They ambled toward the door. Rocky stood hovering over the lawyer, intimidating him in Tito's place.

Hudson was the first to speak. "I've informed Mr. Cox that you are already under NDA for everything seen and heard in this household. Since Cooper is a part of this household, that non-disclosure agreement extends to him. There's no reason he needs to speak to Cooper outside of your protection. As my personal bodyguard, you will be there protecting Cooper." Hudson looked Baker's way. "Ensuring Cooper is completely safe from harm, using any means necessary."

Baker gave Hudson a short nod, accepting the threat for what it was.

Tito held on to Cooper and headed inside. "We'll speak in the kitchen." The large dining room table would keep some distance between Cooper and Baker, making it easier for Tito to keep Cooper safe.

Rocky escorted Baker inside, doubling the threat. Once they were seated across from one another at the table, with Cooper and Tito huddled together on one side and Baker on the other, they were left alone.

· · ·

Baker's expression was oddly kind as his gaze locked on Cooper. "Hey, Cooper. I've been looking for you for a long time."

Cooper didn't respond. His entire body still shook so hard, he nearly gave Tito seasickness.

Baker didn't let Cooper's silence stop him. "I might not have ever found you if not for seeing your photo as part of the news coverage of Hudson's wedding."

"It was a handfasting," Cooper corrected, sounding like a little kid.

A kind smile touched Baker's lips. "I guess that makes sense. How have you been?"

"Why are you here?"

. . .

At Cooper's question, Baker's smile turned sad. "Your father passed."

"How?" Cooper didn't sound upset. He barked every question—like they were forced from his throat.

"He was shot in a mugging gone wrong behind the Angel's Symphony Hall."

Cooper's muscles tensed and relaxed beneath Tito's hold, as if he didn't know how to react. "That was too good of a death for him." The hard edge to Cooper's tone surprised Tito. "Even so, thank you for letting me know."

"That's not really why I'm here," Baker said, refusing to be dismissed. "With your father gone, Quaver Estate is yours as well as all the money earned in his career."

Tito was confused as hell.

. . .

Cooper got angrier by the second. "I don't want it."

Baker didn't back down. "Too bad. It's yours. You have a responsibility to the employees of Quaver."

"No. I don't."

"Claude and Mary are still there."

Cooper went still at Baker's claim. "They are?"

Baker nodded. "Quaver is their home and their livelihood. Personally, I don't care what you do, Cooper. I came here knowing you'll fire me, give away the fifty million, and leave it all behind. No one will blame you, but you can't pretend your responsibilities don't exist. There are real people depending on you."

. . .

While Cooper sat in silence, obviously considering his options, Tito reeled. He had no clue what any of this meant. Apparently, Cooper was worth more than Hudson now. There was an estate with employees. Tito was confused as fuck. No one tried to clarify anything.

Finally, Cooper took an audible breath. "Can I take care of this today?"

Baker smiled. "It's not likely something you can settle all in one day, but you should definitely go to Quaver and get started. The sooner you face everyone, the quicker you can be done with it."

Cooper's body jerked—like something terrible happened to him in his mind. His hold tightened on Tito's hand beneath the table. Tito felt the shaking start again. When Cooper responded, he sounded broken. "I don't know if I can set foot in that house again."

. . .

"Tito will go with you. He'll stay until he brings you back here where you belong," Hudson said from the doorway, proving he had stayed to eavesdrop.

Baker turned in his seat.

Hudson held his stare, showing the side of himself that had kept Tito with him all these years. "Cooper's home is with us. We're his family. I don't really know, nor do I give a fuck what's going on, but I can see you and yours have hurt Cooper enough. We won't stand by and do nothing while you drag him back."

With a dip of his chin, Baker agreed. "Cooper is an adult, and he is also my boss now. He's free to do as he pleases."

Hudson's gaze moved Cooper's way and softened. "We'd like to talk to you about all this when you're ready."

. . .

Rocky and Jinx filled the doorway behind Hudson. They flashed Cooper equally supportive smiles. Tears slipped down Cooper's face. Tito brushed them away.

"What if we make one quick trip today and then try for a longer trip tomorrow?" Baker suggested.

Cooper nodded. "Okay. As long as Tito is with me, I'll be all right."

Tito was awed by Cooper's faith in him. He was still confused and starting to feel like he had been lied to in some way, but it was Cooper. Tito had always known he had secrets.

He stood and helped Cooper to his feet. "We'll follow you."

Cooper said his goodbyes to the guys, promising to explain later before they headed out. They drove in silence. Tito had so many questions, he didn't know where to start. They jumbled in his head. Thirty minutes later, they turned onto a cobblestone driveway that led to a white mansion that sprawled across twice the space of Hudson's place. It was surrounded by beautiful trees and flowers. There was a pond with a pier. Ducks roamed the lawn. Huge columns lined the front porch of the house. Wide red double doors opened as they parked out front.

To Tito's surprise, Cooper immediately stepped out as an elderly man hobbled onto the porch. Tito quickly followed as Cooper jogged up the stairs into the man's waiting arms.

"Claude. Oh, my god. I can't believe you're still here."

The elderly man openly cried as he patted Cooper every place he could reach. "You look so healthy, Coop. I was so worried." He held Cooper's hands and stare. "I never broke. The police were here many times and Kristoff raged, but I never told."

Tears streamed down Cooper's face. "I was terrified he would find out where I got the money to leave. Thank God he never did. I was so scared for you."

Claude hugged Cooper again and steered him inside. "You have to come see Mary."

Baker and Tito followed on their heels. While Claude whisked Cooper away, Tito's feet glued to the floor the moment he stepped inside. The white and black marble floor was only the beginning of the extravagance. Still, the overabundance of wealth wasn't what froze Tito. There was a gigantic oil painting of Cooper standing beside a piano. He was much younger and dressed in the finest of tuxedos. His expression screamed seriousness and there was a deep unhappiness in his eyes.

Tito pointed at the painting. "Is that Cooper?"

. . .

Baker barely spared the canvas a glance. "Yes. Cooper is the greatest child prodigy to ever live, in most experts' opinion. Considering his father was the second richest pianist in the entire world, it was expected of Cooper to also be the best. It's all Cooper's now. Obviously, the money is nowhere near enough to cover the cost of growing up in this house. I should know. I—"

A loud crash came from the direction where Cooper disappeared, and Tito took off running. He shouldn't have let Cooper out of his sight. His heart raced into his throat. He had allowed his shock to render him useless, leaving Cooper unprotected. Tito skidded to a halt at the sight that met him in the next room. Cooper wielded a sledgehammer and had already taken one swing at a grand piano, destroying one of its legs. Claude and an elderly woman Tito assumed was Mary stood in the corner, clapping.

"What in the hell are you doing?"

No one answered Tito.

. . .

Baker made a halting gesture. "At least let me grab you some safety goggles."

Cooper eyed the piano as if it had broken into his home and killed his family. "You're right. This thing has caused enough damage." Cooper's gaze moved to Tito. There was madness in his eyes. He held the sledgehammer out to Tito. "You're bigger than me. Help me destroy this thing."

Tito didn't take the sledgehammer. "Baby, tell me what's going on."

Cooper made an impatient gesture. "Please, Tito. It has to die."

Baker reappeared with a sledgehammer in each hand and three pairs of safety glasses on his head. He passed them out. "We'll take care of this together."

. . .

Despite his horror and confusion, Tito accepted a hammer and joined the destruction. His arms ached and sweat rolled down his back as splinters flew in every direction. By the time the piece was nothing more than a broken mess in the floor, Cooper's hair was plastered with sweat, and blood rolled down his cheek.

Tito's chest heaved as he stared at Cooper. Cooper looked like a different person. Gone was his sweet angel. An angry warrior stood in his place.

Mary touched Cooper's arm. "Let me clean that cut."

As she led Cooper away, Tito broke. He had seen, heard, and done enough with no answers. "Someone tell me what in the fuck is going on here?"

Claude met Tito's stare as he followed Mary and Cooper to the door. His expression spoke volumes. He was a man who had witnessed too much.

"Nightmares live in this house. With any luck, Cooper has come to burn the place to the ground so the evil here can return to the devil who built it."

"Here, here," Baker said, setting his sledgehammer aside. "I could use a drink. How about you, Tito?"

Tito thought he needed more than a drink, but he would take what he could get. He felt like he had fallen down the rabbit hole. Maybe liquor would clear his head.

Nothing felt real. Yet everything that meant the most to him felt like it was slipping away. Cooper had gotten little accomplished beyond promising Claude and Mary they would be taken care of, collecting the debit and credit cards for all the accounts that were now his, and destroying the most poisonous item in his life. Also, Cooper was pretty sure he had destroyed any chance of Tito ever loving him. There was so much ugly beneath his surface. Cooper had really hoped he could stay hidden forever. All

Cooper wanted was to go back to being a nobody guest in Hudson's home. He wanted his only past to be a homeless teen—like he didn't exist before those two years on the street.

Ten minutes from Hudson's house, Tito pulled to the side of the road and killed the engine. To be honest, Tito had lasted much longer than Cooper expected before breaking. It wasn't like Cooper could avoid this. Tito had seen the ugliness, and now he was done.

Cooper wouldn't make Tito say the words. He grabbed the door handle. "I understand. You don't have to tell me to go."

Tito locked the door before Cooper could get out. "What are you talking about?"

Cooper shrugged. "You can boot me from your life now. I know it's what I deserve."

. . .

Tito rubbed his temples. "You're not going anywhere," Tito said, sounding unmistakably angry. "But you have to tell me what in the fuck is going on."

Cooper swiped his hands on his jeans. "I don't really know where to start."

"Try starting at the beginning," Tito snapped. "Jinx said you were homeless because your mom had kicked you out for being gay. Now you have more money and twice the house as Hudson. I don't understand. I need the truth."

"I'm the son of Kristoff Whitaker."

Tito blinked. "Why do I know that name?" Before Cooper could answer, Tito's expression cleared. "Wait. Baker said your dad was a pianist. Was he that rich guy who stabbed his wife to death and got away with it?"

· · ·

Cooper knew they would never be the same now. No one wanted the son of a murderer in their home. "Yes."

Tito looked away and stared at nothing. "Holy shit." He visibly swallowed before looking back Cooper's way. "How did you end up homeless?"

"After my mom's murder, Claude helped me run away."

"Did he actually kill your mom? People were pretty divided over it since the charges were dropped and the ruling was sealed."

Cooper shrugged. "I don't know. I had my first concert in New York that night, so I wasn't home when she died. But Dad was... evil. Sadistic. He had no qualms about torturing us in every way possible while shaping us into who he wanted us to be. I'd say he was definitely capable of murder."

. . .

A muscle in Tito's jaw flexed. "And the piano?"

Tito deserved an explanation after helping Cooper destroy it. "He used to make me sit at that piano eighteen hours a day to practice. I was expected to be perfect so I wouldn't embarrass him. If I didn't make a single mistake all day, I was allowed an hour of chess and tutoring with Claude and one meal. If a single note went wrong..." Cooper's voice died. He couldn't relive those nights of horror. Cooper unconsciously traced the spot on his leg where his jeans hid one of his many scars. He lost himself to a nightmare. Maybe he had never been saved from that place. The horrors still lived in his head.

Tito reached over and took his hand. "You're right. Getting shot during a mugging gone wrong was too good for him. I'll explain everything to Hudson and the guys. You need some rest. After I talk to Hudson, I'll bring you something to eat."

Cooper nodded. Everything hurt, and he wasn't ready to face lying to everyone about how he had ended up homeless. Life was easier when people didn't know he was completely broken. When Cooper had run away from Quaver, he had chosen a new past for himself. One he could live with. Now he had to explain why he had lied. Cooper didn't know if he could.

Tito pulled back into traffic and they fell into silence. Maybe they would never have anything to say to each other again. A tear rolled down Cooper's cheek. He wiped it away. When another fell, he looked out the window to keep Tito from seeing. There were years and years of ugliness inside his head. Two years of living in the street was nothing. Since Rocky took him in, Cooper had tried to be someone new. He wanted to reinvent himself. To survive himself, Cooper needed to let his past die the obscure death it deserved. He had been in a great place mentally lately, thanks to Tito. Cooper could feel that new strength crumbling.

The moment Tito stopped the car outside Hudson's house, Cooper was out the door. He hurried inside and up the stairs before anyone saw the tears he couldn't keep inside. The moment he shut himself inside his room, Cooper spiraled. Soon the people he had fallen in love with would know everything. Tito would tell them all about Cooper's ugly life and everything would change. Every time they set eyes on him, he would be Kristoff Whitaker's son. He would be Cooper Whitaker, the child tortured into following in the footsteps of one of the greatest pianists in the world. All Cooper had ever wanted for himself was to be free. While homeless, he had suffered, but it had been nothing compared to the nightmare he had left behind. Now everyone he loved knew it.

Cooper's mind raged like a category five hurricane. Memories whipped at his brain, trying to kill him. Tears poured down his face unchecked. A scream built in his throat with nowhere to go. His sanity needed him to act. Cooper grabbed the suitcases he had just unpacked from their trip. He opened drawers and slung things inside before he realized it would be too hard to climb out a second-story window with suitcases. His backpack would have to sustain him, the way it had the night he had run away from Quaver. Cooper grabbed the same things Claude had given him: his ID, passport, and one change of clothes. He didn't have any food in his bedroom he could take. At least this time he had the debit cards Baker had given him today. He could go to a hotel and plan his next stop. Maybe he could go back to Ibiza for a while. Cooper could bask in the happy memories he had made there while he came to terms with his past. With his backpack half on, Cooper froze. His mind cleared a hair. He had made happy memories here too.

The bedroom door opened, and Rocky's large frame filled the doorway. He eyed the tears streaming down Cooper's face and the backpack hanging from Cooper's arm. His expression gave nothing away. Rocky's long stride ate up the space between them. He grabbed the backpack and tossed it aside before towing Cooper into the safety of his bear-sized embrace. The world went silent. All Cooper could hear was the sound of Rocky's heart beating while tears flowed like he had an endless supply. Cooper hadn't cried in years. Crying had always made the beatings worse. His father had wanted him to be mentally and physically tough. If he didn't cry, the pain ended faster. The truth hit him. Subconsciously, Cooper had known he was safe here. He hadn't even thought about his tears other than thinking he didn't want anyone's pity. No one under this roof would hurt him or think badly of him. Cooper trusted them. He needed them.

Warm bodies surrounded him. Cooper found himself the center of a group hug. He let their strength hold him together. God knew, he had nothing left to give.

FOUR

WITH HIS MIND trapped in the day's horror, Tito arranged the food he ordered for Cooper on a tray. At the last second, he grabbed the first-aid kit too. He hadn't inspected the cut on Cooper's face yet. No doubt Mary was used to tending to Cooper's wounds, but Tito needed to see to it himself. His insides shook with anger and fear. Tito wanted to dig up Kristoff and kill him again. He was also scared as hell Cooper wouldn't go back to being the Cooper he loved. Maybe it was a ridiculous fear, but Tito had fallen in love with a sweet homeless kid with a mysterious past. Now Cooper was the wealthy son of a world-renowned pianist, and Tito was just a bodyguard. Tito stared at nothing while losing himself. Everything felt like an act. He didn't know what was real anymore.

Rocky squeezed his shoulder, pulling him from his depressing thoughts. "This looks good. In case I haven't said so before, I really appreciate the way you always take care of him. Cooper needs exactly what you give him."

"He's worth fifty-two million. I'm not sure he needs anyone." Tito felt like an asshole as soon as the words left his mouth. They were true, though.

Rocky scowled. "Don't start that shit. I went down a similar path when I learned Hudson is bipolar. I thought I wasn't enough and not what he needed. Idiotic thoughts like that almost ruined the best things in my life. Cooper is still Cooper. He leans on you and looks at you like you're the original creator of happiness. Everything you learned today means next to nothing, if you think about it. Cooper walked away from that life. You saw the way he shook at the idea of going back. He needs you more than ever with this ugly past being shoved down his throat against his will. Cooper wants to be who he is with us. Help him hang on to it."

Rocky was right. Cooper was terrified of being forced to walk a path he didn't choose. He had survived evil. Tito would never let anyone drag Cooper back to that nightmare. "How is he?"

Rocky shook his head. His pinched features didn't give Tito much hope. "He just got in the shower, but he hasn't stopped crying. This is hard for me to watch. When I met Cooper, he was a defiant and mouthy teenager. I didn't know this was what that mask hid. He really needs you, Tito. If one day of revisiting the past leaves him like this, I can't even imagine what'll become of him if this lawyer drags him back to that life."

Tito grabbed the tray to stop himself from punching the wall. He held the wooden board in a much tighter grip than necessary. "No one is making Cooper do anything on my watch."

Rocky eyed him, as if searching for something only he could see. He gave Tito a sharp nod. "Good. You should get back to him. When I went to his room earlier, he was packing to run away again."

A shot of outrage hit Tito. He stepped around Rocky and stormed to Cooper's room. Even though Tito realized he should have seen that one coming, he was still outraged. How dare Cooper try to leave him? They were supposed to be friends. More than friends. Goddamn it. Cooper fucked with his head. Tito burst into Cooper's room, ready to come unglued over Cooper's runaway attempt.

Cooper stepped from the bathroom, looking like he might fall apart any second. His eyes were red, and he seemed even smaller than usual. His wet blond hair stood in every direction. The cut on his face made Tito's heart squeeze. Someone had hurt his baby when Tito hadn't been around yet to help. He wanted to kill someone. That wasn't an option. All he could do was be here now.

"Do you think you can eat something?"

Cooper didn't spare the food a glance. His gaze never wavered from holding Tito's stare. "Do you think you'll ever look at me again and not see a broken mess? I kind of miss that already."

Tito's heart broke at the way Cooper's voice shook, as if trying to give out. He quickly set the tray aside and closed the distance between them. "You are *not* broken." Even Tito heard the rage in his voice as he bent and claimed Cooper's mouth.

Cooper went wild beneath Tito's touch, as if Tito was exactly what he needed to feel whole again. Cooper tugged at Tito's shirt until his hands found bare skin. A stuttered breath escaped Tito. He had never wanted anyone as much as he did Cooper. On paper, it seemed wrong. Cooper was eleven years younger than him. He was in a vulnerable place and Tito knew better. In reality, they were perfect together. Tito had never felt so right with anyone. Their conversations were never stilted. Their silence was never heavy. They felt meant to be. Tito didn't feel like he took advantage of Cooper. Cooper led. Tito always only went where Cooper let him go. Tonight was no different.

"Make love to me the way you did in Ibiza. I want to go back to when everything felt perfect."

Cooper didn't need to ask twice. Tito would do whatever it took to pull Cooper from the edge. This was love. Tito would heal him. He swept Cooper from his feet and headed for the bed. There was a world of lovemaking Cooper hadn't been introduced to yet, but tonight wasn't the night. Tonight was about making Cooper forget any life he had before Tito. Tito planned to be his future.

"Tell me if I go too far," Tito said as he set Cooper on the bed and followed him down.

. . .

Cooper looked innocent and vulnerable as he stared up at Tito. That didn't stop Tito from peeling off his shirt and stealing Cooper's too. Once they were bare from the waist up, Tito reclaimed Cooper's mouth. Nothing he learned today changed a goddamn thing. Tito felt how he felt.

To his surprise, Cooper unbuttoned Tito's pants. Every muscle in Tito's body tensed with pleasure as Cooper's hand dove inside. Tito decided to try to go a bit further than planned. "Is it okay if we get rid of these clothes? As much as I don't mind coming in my pants for you, I want to feel your skin against mine."

"Okay."

At the trust in Cooper's voice, Tito moved slow. He kissed any part of Cooper he could reach while removing each article of clothing. Tito needed Cooper aroused enough to stay distracted. Once they were nude and Tito's body covered Cooper's, something inside Tito clicked. He swore they had been made for each other. There was no other way to explain the way Tito felt when they were together. He had been with countless men. This was the one he wanted.

"Tito." The breathless whisper nearly crippled Tito.

"I'm here, baby." As Tito made the vow, he rocked against Cooper's body. With their erections trapped between them, the friction had Tito sucking in a sharp breath. It was crazy how such a vanilla act fucked so hard with his head. He could make love to Cooper all day, but Cooper felt too good beneath him.

"I wish you really wanted me. There's nothing I want more than for you to want to be with me for real and not out of pity."

Rage slapped Tito so hard, he saw red. He froze and stared down at Cooper like they had never met. The tears he saw in Cooper's eyes immediately killed Tito's fury. He fought to think of a single thing he had done or said to make Cooper think this wasn't real. Nothing came to mind. All Tito deduced was maybe he hadn't said enough. "You can't really be that blind."

Cooper blinked rapidly at Tito's words. Tears rolled back into Cooper's hair. "What do you mean?"

A sardonic smile touched Tito's lips. He had truly failed Cooper. "This is real. You're the only person I want. I thought you knew you're mine."

Cooper bit his bottom lip—like he was scared to hope. "Are you mine?"

A smile exploded across Tito's face. "Every second of the day."

. . .

"Oh." The wonderment in that single word had Tito taking a breath. Everything about Cooper was completely guileless. It was intoxicating to be wanted by someone so unassuming. Tito hoped Cooper never changed.

While holding Cooper's stare, Tito slowly lowered his head. This time, when their lips met, Tito was fully focused on satisfaction. He needed Cooper to come back for more. Tito wanted everything. Cooper released a small gasp when Tito rolled his hips. That wasn't good enough. Tito wanted Cooper wild with lust. He reached between their bodies and palmed their cocks. Cooper's fingernails dug into Tito's skin. Tito stroked, finding his rhythm. Cooper whimpered against Tito's lips. Tito kissed a path to Cooper's ear and licked. He pumped faster while focusing on the building tension. Words spilled from Tito without thought.

"Goddamn, Cooper. One of these days, I'll make love to you for real. I plan to tease you first, though. You need to be ready for me. I want to be inside you."

. . .

"Oh, god."

The whisper had Tito on the verge of losing control. Cooper was an addiction. Tito had spent too many nights fantasizing. He was so close to blowing. "Come for me, Cooper. Soak my skin and make me clean up a mess. I want your cum coating my fingers."

Rapid panting sounded against Tito's ear. Tito pumped faster. A strangled cry rent the air. Cum filled Tito's hand and the space between them. Tito saw stars as an orgasm ripped from him, stealing all the air from the room. He cried out against Cooper's shoulder. There was a mess between them, and Tito didn't care. He needed to taste Cooper's lips. Their tongues stroked and their hearts pounded, trying to get closer to each other. Tito knew beyond a shadow of a doubt that Cooper was his future. They just needed to figure out the present first.

Cooper stared into the dark while Tito held him. Without Tito, Cooper would have fallen completely apart. When he left Quaver estate over two years ago, Cooper had planned to never return. Today, all the ugliness had roared back to swallow him whole. Cooper didn't want to lose himself. Then, as always, Tito had saved him. In what should have been one of the worst days of his life, Tito had said they were together. Cooper hadn't dared to dream. He wanted to stay completely focused on them, but the day kept pushing its way in.

"I don't want to go back."

Tito stroked Cooper's stomach, letting Cooper know he listened. As always, he let Cooper work things through.

"I have to, though. Claude and Mary deserve that much."

. . .

"Claude said he hopes you burn the place to the ground."

"I honestly don't know what to do," Cooper said, admitting the only thing he knew for sure. "It's easy to say I want nothing from my dad, but does it make me a bad person because I also feel entitled to everything? I paid in blood for every penny."

Tito moved up onto his elbow to hold Cooper's stare. He didn't respond right away. It was obvious he took Cooper's question seriously. "To my way of thinking, the hows and whys don't matter. Whether you want it or are entitled to it, everything that was his is yours now. You have the world at your fingertips. If you want, you could set Claude and Mary up for life, sell the property, and give everything to charity." Tito's expression turned sad. "Or you can embrace your new fortune and leave everything behind. I guess that includes me."

Everything inside Cooper screamed in denial. He could not lose Tito. That wasn't an option. "So you're saying if I decide to keep this money, then we're over?"

Tito's eyebrows snapped together into a deep scowl. "No. I guess I'm just realizing how completely out of my league you are. The moment you embrace the life of a rich socialite, I'll be just some lowly bodyguard you used to know."

A snort burst from Cooper. "I don't think making one point five million a year guarding the biggest name in alt rock is a lowly job."

Tito's expression cleared. A smile touched his lips. "How do you know how much I make?"

Guilt had Cooper's gaze sliding away. "Sorry. I'm quiet and observant. People talk around me without thinking. It's like I disappear in the background."

. . .

Tito stroked Cooper's stomach. "Don't apologize. I don't care if you know how much I make. It's not really about money. It's about station. People will accept you into the fold of the rich and elite. It wouldn't be fair of me to hold you back."

An ugly thought wormed its way inside Cooper's head. "Are you trying to dump me by making it sound like it's in my best interest?"

One incredulous look from Tito made Cooper feel like shit for suggesting Tito would do anything so shady. "You're mine. Nothing could change how I feel." Tito's irritation disappeared. His gaze slid away, but not before Cooper saw the hurt that he tried hiding. "I'm just saying I won't hold you back. If you decide you need to find yourself, I'll be here waiting."

Cooper wished he could make Tito understand. There was no way he would let his dad steal anything else from him, especially Tito. He just needed to figure out what to do next. "Whatever I choose, I still need you. This money changes nothing. You're my best friend. I can't lose you."

A sexy smirk touched Tito's lips. "Damn right, you can't. I'd hate to have to stalk you."

Cooper laughed. Tito was ridiculous. He knew Tito would never stoop to becoming the same type of person he protected Hudson from all these years. It was a nice thought, though, thinking Tito might like him that much.

"Will you stay with me?"

Tito's smile slipped away. His expression turned dark and possessive. "I'm not going anywhere."

Cooper prayed that was true. He had a feeling nothing good would come of dealing with his dad's estate. Kristoff Whitaker's evil tainted everything. God knew Cooper had no hope of washing away the scars. All he could do was hope Tito never realized exactly how fucked up Cooper really was, because Cooper was completely in love with Tito. He hadn't stood a chance of not falling. Tito was the hero in Cooper's story. Cooper wasn't a hundred percent certain he wasn't the villain. After all, he was his father's son. Maybe evil wasn't something he could escape.

FIVE

TITO WOKE UP SMILING. He was still a bit scared about losing Cooper to his new life, but mostly, he was just happy. They were on the same page. They were a couple now. It was hard as hell not to make eyes at Cooper all morning across the breakfast table. His open desire to have Cooper alone came to a screeching halt when Hudson stepped in, touching Tito's shoulder to get his attention.

"I'd like to have a word with you in my studio when you're ready."

Cooper shot Tito a worried look.

. . .

Tito winked as he stood. "I'm at your disposal."
Even though Tito tried blowing things off for
Cooper's sake, Tito worried dating Cooper might go
too far for Hudson. Despite Hudson knowing Tito
had feelings for Cooper, they hadn't really
discussed what would happen if Tito moved on
those feelings. Tito got the impression he was about
to find out. He followed Hudson into the studio.
Hudson picked up a guitar and strummed a few
notes. Tito had always been wowed by Hudson. He
was a musical genius. There wasn't an instrument
he couldn't play without having to take a single
lesson. It was as if music flowed from him, giving
the instruments life. Tito had always seen what the
rest of the world saw when they looked at Hudson.
He was magic.

Tito snagged a stool from behind the drums and sat.
"What's up?"

Hudson leaned on the guitar and met Tito's stare.
"The guys and I were up all night, talking. I'm not

touring anymore, and I have other guards. Plus, Rocky has worked in security for years."

"Are you firing me?"

Hudson looked horrified at Tito's sudden question. "No. You're like family to me. This is your home. I am reassigning you, though. To watching Cooper. He needs you full-time, I think. With this new fortune will come new dangers. You know how it is."

Tito nodded. "Yeah. I talked to him about it a little last night." Tito scratched his nose. He was too honest. Tito couldn't let Hudson pay him for dating Cooper. "There's a slight problem with what you're asking. Cooper and I are dating."

Hudson snorted. "No shit. I'm not an idiot. You two are always looking at each other like you're each other's next meal. But I trust you to be professional. I know you'll do your job no matter how you feel. After all, you've been with me for years and I love you like a brother. That's never impeded your work. If anything, it's made you better at your job. I know you'd never let anything happen to me. You'd also never let anything happen to Cooper. He needs you more than I do right now."

Tito nodded. Everything Hudson said was true. Tito would die for Hudson and Cooper. He would protect them with his last breath. Still, there were a few holes in this plan. "What if Cooper decides to move out?"

Hudson shrugged. "Then I guess we'll cross that bridge when we get there. I can't imagine that'll happen tomorrow. Cooper isn't ready to be alone. You and I both know it. I get the feeling Cooper knows it too."

A light tapping on the doorframe brought Tito's head around. Cooper stood just outside the doorway, looking unsure of his welcome. "Is it okay if I join you? Rocky told me you're swapping Tito's duties to sticking with me. I just want to make sure I haven't gotten him in trouble."

Hudson waved Cooper inside. "Not at all. I'm retired now and a newlywed. It just makes sense for Tito to keep you safe since Rocky lives here now."

Cooper sat behind the keyboard. A bright smile lit his face. "You won't hear me complain about Tito being glued to my side."

With a chuckle, Hudson strummed one of his older songs on the guitar. It was obvious he did it on autopilot without paying attention. Cooper played with the keys on the keyboard and adjusted the sound, automatically matching Hudson. He stopped, pulled a face, and then slowed down the song.

"Drop a key and slow down," Cooper said absently.

.   .   .

Hudson did as Cooper suggested, making a head-banging song into a dark, almost ominous tune.

Tito sat, stunned by Cooper's talent. By ear, he created a new and amazing version of Hudson's song. Hudson nodded toward the microphone, and Tito adjusted the stand so Hudson could sing. Tito was moved. The new song was deep and would—no doubt—be a hit. That thought had Tito moving to the booth and hitting the record button. He had shadowed Hudson for so many years, he could do almost any tech job Hudson needed. When the song ended, they immediately started again from the top, working seamlessly together to perfect their creation. The next time, they seemed happier with the outcome. When the final notes died, Hudson and Cooper smiled at each other like they had found their musical soul mates.

"We should release that. Hell, I think we should redo a whole album slowed down."

. . .

Cooper blushed. "You don't have to flatter me. I know I'm not my dad."

Tito couldn't believe Cooper didn't see how rare his talent was. People didn't walk into a studio and just create something new with Hudson fucking Vincent.

Thankfully, Hudson didn't let it go. "No. You're not your dad. You're you, and that was amazing. Seriously, let's collaborate on something."

"I thought you were retired."

Hudson nodded. "I am. That means I can work on whatever I want without the pressure. It's something we can just do in our spare time."

While Cooper's cheeks were still pink, he made Tito proud by not letting his embarrassment stand in the way. "Okay. If you really want to play around some more, I'm in."

. . .

Hudson set his guitar aside. "Cool. We can talk about it after dinner tonight, if that's okay. Rocky has to work today, so Jinx and I plan to hang out by the pool. Do you two want to join us?"

Cooper's beautiful green gaze moved Tito's way. A smile lit his face. "Thanks for the offer, but no. Tito is teaching me how to surf."

It looked like they were headed to Surfrider beach. Tito liked this plan. Brent appeared in the doorway with a stack of envelopes in hand.

"Sorry to interrupt, but like twenty invitations to tonight's events have been hand-delivered this morning."

Hudson shrugged. "You know the drill. Toss them in the trash."

. . .

Brent shifted from foot to foot, looking uncomfortable. "They're for Cooper."

All eyes turned Cooper's way. Cooper spent a moment visibly floundering before his spine stiffened. He looked Brent's way. "If it's not any trouble, will you just toss them in the trash?"

Brent's eyebrows rose. Like Tito, he understood what Cooper turned down. Each party would be one for the record books. All the alcohol, drugs, and blow jobs Cooper could ever want waited for him on the other side.

"Are you sure?"

Cooper nodded at Brent's question. "Please. If any more show up, you can just toss those too. Thank you."

. . .

Even though Tito was completely in love with Cooper and grateful he didn't plan to join the social elite, he also understood what Cooper was missing. "Are you positive? You'd probably have a blast."

Cooper met Tito's stare and smiled. "Yes. Stop worrying about me. I have dinner plans here with the alt rock god and a surfing lesson today. That's the life I want. I know a good thing when I see it, and I already have the best. The party life isn't for me."

Tito knew a good thing too, and he wouldn't push. He recognized Cooper chose him. He wouldn't let Cooper regret it. "I guess we'd better head out, then. We need to stop at one of the surf shops and get you some gear. You'll need it if we plan to do this a few days a week."

Cooper jumped to his feet, looking ready to clap his hands in his excitement. "Yay. I'll go get ready."

. . .

When Cooper disappeared, Tito dared a glance Hudson's way. Hudson eyed him like a proud father, even though Hudson was only two years older than him. "You're a good man."

Tito fought a blush at Hudson's praise. He hoped that was true. Tito always tried his best. Still, there was more to it than that. Tito couldn't stop himself from admitting as much. "Honestly, I'm just completely in love."

Hudson pulled a face. "I know. He's really young, though. I hope you don't get hurt."

Yeah. Tito did too.

The board bobbed beneath them. Sitting face to face, Cooper stared into Tito's eyes. He was happier in that moment than he had ever been. They stopped at a locally owned surf shop earlier and bought Cooper a surf suit. He had also picked up a tandem board as well as one he could ride alone if he got brave enough. Tito had picked up some odds and ends Cooper would need if he planned to keep up this hobby. When it came time to pay, Cooper had experienced a huge sense of pride to be the one who settled the bill. Everyone had been carrying him for months. Even though no one complained, Cooper liked knowing he could buy whatever he wanted now. He could be the one who spoiled his friends.

After hours of practice and Cooper managing twice to ride a wave alone, he soaked up the isolation of sitting with Tito in the water. No one could hear them. It was like they were in their own bubble. That was one of the biggest reasons Cooper kept working at the sport. He enjoyed having Tito all to himself. The isolation of the ocean seemed the perfect spot for confessions.

"I've decided to sign Quaver over to Claude and Mary. They can do what they want with it. I also asked Baker to cut them a hefty check. They were more like parents to me than my real parents. I can't leave them high and dry, but neither can I go back to living at Quaver."

Tito nodded. "It sounds like you've been thinking things through with a level head."

He had. Cooper had stayed awake almost the entire night, watching Tito sleep while thinking about what he wanted to do with his future and newfound wealth. "Yeah. I did some soul-searching last night. There's nothing I can do with this money that'll undo every bad thing my dad did. So I've decided to give half the money to various charities and keep the rest. I don't know what to do with my future yet, but I know I can't expect Hudson to take care of me forever."

A bright smile lit Tito's face before a sexy chuckle rumbled from his chest. "Actually, you can. Once Hudson adopts someone, he takes care of them for life, but I get what you're saying. No one wants to ask for every little thing they want. It's good to have your own money. Do you have something you want out of life—like a dream?"

Cooper tried not to blush, but he couldn't quite hold Tito's gaze. "If you'd asked me that yesterday, I would've said no." Excitement had him meeting Tito's stare again. "But this morning was so much fun. Hudson and I made a great team. If he's really serious about collaborating on an album, that would be like a dream come true." Cooper's smile fell as reality washed over him. "I never wanted to play a single note again when I ran away from Quaver. I'm not sure what came over me this morning. The keyboard was right there while I listened to Hudson mindlessly playing his guitar. It was like I couldn't stop myself."

"From what I have heard so far about your dad, he's likely spinning in his grave at the idea of you playing grunge rock, so don't sweat it."

Cooper hadn't thought of that. A laugh burst from him at the thought of his dad's face, if he knew.

Good. Cooper hoped he was roasting in hell and watching Cooper thrive. There was no better revenge.

Tito glanced toward the shore. "I guess we should head back in if we want to be home in time to have dinner with the guys."

Cooper nodded. "In a minute." With a burst of unexpected bravery, Cooper lured Tito closer and stole a quick kiss. Tito's expression turned so heated so fast that Cooper made a mental note to be brave more often.

"Damn. You're sexy."

Cooper blinked. He had never thought of himself as being considered sexy. It was nice. Being with Tito was the best decision Cooper had ever made. He was good for Cooper in every way. Cooper's mental health and happiness level had never been so high. Tito would never understand how much Cooper loved and appreciated him. Sometimes, Cooper wished he had the courage to tell Tito, but that was too big of a risk. They had just started dating. Tito wasn't ready to hear how obsessed Cooper was with him. They swam back to shore with their boards. At the edge of the parking lot, they were met with a huge crowd of people carrying cameras and microphones.

Tito switched to guard mode while Cooper tried understanding what happened. People screamed questions at him about his mother's murder and his dad's recent death. Someone else asked about his recent fortune while another guy asked where Cooper had been hiding the last couple of years. Cooper knew he looked as stunned as he felt, but Tito had things under control. He used his inhuman size and the tandem board to keep the reporters at bay. Tito shuffled Cooper inside the SUV and locked the doors before closing Cooper inside. He handled the crowd while strapping their boards to the roof. By the time Tito climbed behind the wheel, his expression was hard and closed, making Cooper's oncoming panic attack worse. He needed to get away. Cooper hadn't felt like this in years. He needed to go somewhere dark where no one could look at him.

"What is happening?" Even Cooper heard the breathless panic in his voice.

Tito squeezed the steering wheel as he drove. His constant mirror checking had Cooper's panic doubling. "I don't know. The socialite invitations were something I expected, but this is nuts. Don't worry, though. I've got you."

"How did they know where to find me?"

Tito shook his head. "I don't know. These people are sneaky. All it takes is one lead and they're like ants on spilled soda." He dug his Bluetooth from the console and put the earpiece in. "I have to call security at the house and make sure they're ready. I'll get Brent to meet us at the gate."

. . .

Cooper didn't want to live the rest of his life like this. He had just found a certain level of freedom and normalcy. Cooper wasn't strong enough for this much negative attention. The overwhelming need to disappear choked Cooper. He felt like he was under the watchful eye of his dad all over again. Expectations were toxic to Cooper. Failure came at too high of a price. In his panic, Cooper completely missed the drive. Unfortunately, there was no missing the huge crowd of reporters outside Hudson's gate.

"Oh my god. I'm so sorry. Hudson just retired and I'm disrupting his life. I can't believe this is happening."

Tito didn't respond. He looked as if his entire concentration was on getting Cooper inside the gates and house unaccosted. Brent opened Cooper's door the second they were inside the safety of the gate.

Tito pointed toward the house. "Take him to my room and stay with him until I get there. I have to check with the gate guards to make sure they stay on high alert."

Brent nodded and walked Cooper inside. The stress was too much. His mind retreated behind the same wall it built to survive his dad. There was too much happening. He was in overload. One thought remained clear. He would never be allowed to find peace. It was like his dad punished him from the beyond the grave. Cooper didn't know if he could live with that.

Tito was enraged. He had no idea how the press had found them while surfing or why they had pounced in the first place. He had known the coverage of Cooper's mom's murder had been extensive, but Tito had never expected that it would blow up again with Kristoff's death. It seemed the violent death of a murderer was big business for the media. Unfortunately, Cooper would pay the price for a while. Like all things, this would be old news one day. Tito didn't know how long this craziness would last, but he had to keep Cooper safe.

. . .

Poor Cooper. Tito couldn't get Cooper's shocked expression out of his mind. This new development had obviously floored him. Tito fucking hated it. With the front gate security dealt with, Tito headed for the house. He needed to keep Cooper calm. Cooper had to know this was only temporary. Tito raced up the stairs. Brent stood outside Tito's bedroom, guarding the door. Tito didn't expect the press to storm the house. He expected Cooper to bolt. Cooper didn't handle stress well, and this definitely fell under the high anxiety umbrella.

Tito gave Brent a sharp nod as he headed inside the room. It was empty. Tito raced to the bathroom. Cooper's wetsuit was on the bathroom floor. Otherwise, it was empty. Tito jetted toward the hall. Brent hadn't made it to the elevator yet.

Tito pointed toward his bedroom. "Where did he go?"

. . .

Horror passed over Brent's features. "Nowhere. He went in and didn't come out. Should I search the property?"

Tito waved off the suggestion. He didn't think Cooper would sneak out in the nude. "Not yet. I must've missed him." Tito went back into his room and tried to think. His room was large, but not so large he could lose a whole person. Tito checked under the bed. There was no one there. The balcony door locked with a key and it was still locked. As his panicked gaze skimmed the room, he noticed his closet door was slightly ajar. Tito crossed the room and looked inside. He found Cooper sitting on the floor in the dark, wearing nothing but one of Tito's t-shirts. The material swallowed him whole. With his knees pulled up inside the shirt, he had his arms wrapped around his legs, looking ready to cry.

"I'm not crazy."

. . .

Tito fought a smile. His poor angel. He turned on the light and stepped inside the closet. "I know. You're overwhelmed. I get it."

Cooper buried his face in the shirt—like a turtle, trying even harder to hide, as if the closet wasn't a small enough space. Tito moved to the back of the closet and found a huge plastic tote he brought with him when he moved in. His grandmother had passed away when Tito was seventeen. He had spent a lot of time with her growing up. She had always told him he was secretly her favorite. Tito had loved hanging out with her. Sewing had been her passion, and she was always making things for Tito, even after he had outgrown toys. He had kept every single thing she had made for him over the years. Tito was thankful for that now. He found a squishy and super soft teddy bear she had made for him and moved to sit at Cooper's side.

"My nonna made this for me like a month before she died. I think she would love knowing I gave it to you."

. . .

Cooper uncovered his face. His eyes filled with wonderment as he reached for the bear. "He's adorable. Thank you." He hugged it to his chest. His eyes moved toward the tote. "What else do you have in there?"

Cooper's curiosity made Tito smile. Tito saw his chance to distract Cooper. First, he had to get out of his wetsuit. Under Cooper's watchful gaze, Tito peeled off the suit and tossed it outside the closet. He grabbed a pair of boxer briefs and pulled them on before closing them inside the walk-in closet again. Tito could feel Cooper's gaze following his every move. He knew Cooper wanted him. Always had. Cooper wore his every emotion openly. He made Tito feel like he could take over the world. No one had ever made Tito feel so powerful. It was addicting.

Tito grabbed the tote and carried it to Cooper's side. "My nonna used to do a lot of sewing. I stayed with her during every school break growing up. She used to dote on me, and she made me a ton of stuff over the years. This is just some of it." Tito sat on the opposite side of the tote while Cooper dove in. Each item was sealed in a plastic bag. Cooper opened each one, inspecting it. Halfway in, Cooper was surrounded by stuffed animals, Tito wore a cape that went with a Halloween costume Nonna had made for him, and Cooper inspected another costume she had made him for Pride. It was full of rainbow colors.

Tito explained the outfit. "She used to make all of my family outfits for Pride each year. We went as a family. She was my biggest supporter."

Cooper looked floored. "Your whole family went to Pride? That's amazing. I can hear the love in your voice when you talk about them."

Tito nodded. "They're great. My parents, Tricia and Dante, have been married forty years this year. Anna, my baby sister, is married with twin boys. My older brothers, Enzo and Marco, are both pilots in the Navy. We're a big Italian family. Loud and loving."

. . .

With the bear hugged to his chest, Cooper leaned against the wall. "Have you had a happy life?"

He didn't need to think about it. "Yeah, it's been pretty good. I mean, siblings fight and whatnot, but we love each other. I came out of high school a big, buff guy and landed this dream job right away." A smile exploded across his face. "Eleven years with Hudson has been wild as hell. It's been a good life."

Cooper's gaze dropped to his lap. He toyed with the bear. "My life was nothing like that."

Tito hated that. He wanted to hear there had been at least one good thing. "What was your mom like?"

Cooper's shoulder lifted in a half shrug. For a moment, he plucked at the bear and Tito didn't think he would answer. When he did, he sounded bitter. "Weak. Dad would've never married anyone who upstaged him. She just kind of melted into the background of every room. I guess I'm just like her."

Before Tito could find the words to argue, Cooper kept talking. "The day Dad... the day she died, that was the only time I had ever seen her stand up to him. I had just gotten my passport, and they took me to the airport for my first concert. Dad was planning my life, talking about how I would travel the world, living up to his name. Even though I was thrilled to be getting a taste of freedom, I was also terrified because Dad said I had to go alone. I had to learn to be strong and independent because I was a star. Mom snapped. I'd never seen her angry, but she was furious he would send me across the country to New York alone. She said anything could happen to me." A caustic-looking smile touched Cooper's lips. "This coming from the woman who stood aside my whole life while everything had already happened to me." For a long moment, Cooper stared at Tito in silence. When he spoke, his voice sounded dead in a way that broke Tito's heart. "I don't want a loud, wild life. My entire life has been filled with shouting and anger. Pain. Now I just want peace. I understand if the drama of paparazzi and partying is what makes you happy. You're different from me. Stronger than me. I just need life to be quiet and let me rest. I'm fucking tired, Tito." Cooper's final words came out in a passionate whisper, tearing at Tito's heart. Maybe

Cooper was only eighteen, but his life had been long and hard. He was older than Tito in his soul.

Tito had to be honest about his energy level too. "I don't know how much you know about Hudson, but if you live here long enough, you'll find out. He's bipolar, and when he tours, which used to be all the time, he refuses to stay medicated. For the last eleven years, I've been his twenty-four-seven crisis control center. Don't get me wrong, I love him and a lot of the time he's great. We've had a lot of good times, but I'm exhausted. I've had to be on guard every second of the day, not knowing if he'll step into traffic or down a bottle of pills. He's just not very attached to living, and it's hard work keeping him here. I'm relieved as hell that he's retired and married now. That's not a life I can sustain any longer. It feels like I haven't slept in a decade. I don't want to go back to living in crisis mode again." An expected sardonic laugh escaped Tito. "I really don't want to have to go back to shaving my head bald again."

Cooper leaned his way, looking fascinated. "Why did you have to keep your head shaved bald?"

. . .

"The fucking fans," Tito said, sounding as outraged as he felt. Also, Cooper was smiling, and Tito couldn't stop being outrageous for him. "They would climb me like a fucking tree, using my hair as a grip to climb over me and get to Hudson. You have no idea. People are nuts. They'll do anything for one shot at a fantasy."

Cooper swept Tito with a heated gaze. "I get it. I'd do a lot for a shot at my fantasy too."

The air changed, turning heavy with desire. Tito took off his cape and tossed it aside. "Like what?"

Cooper tapped his chin, as if obnoxiously thinking about it. His eyes lit. "I'd use my new fortune to steal him away to the vacation spot of his choosing. No press. No one looking at me with pity or for answers I don't have. Just us and his wishes come true."

. . .

Tito moved his knees and crawled Cooper's way. "For the record, this him is me, correct?"

Cooper's eyes swam with laughter. "Yes. I'm talking about you."

Tito kept moving until he had Cooper within his grasp. "How do you feel about San Diego?"

"I've never been there, but I've heard good things. Why San Diego? It's only like two hours away."

Tito thought it might be best to keep that part to himself for a little while. Plus, he had other plans for Cooper. "We should take a shower."

Cooper licked his lips. "Tito, I have a lot of scars and—"

. . .

Tito kissed him. He didn't want to hear it. Tito had already seen Cooper's scars on the sly. He had done his best to let Cooper keep his pride, but Tito was in this for the long haul. Eventually, Cooper would have to let him in. "You're beautiful. Come, take a shower with me," Tito cajoled between kisses. He toyed with Cooper's tongue, seducing him. With Cooper distracted, Tito quickly stood with Cooper in his arms. He was so light; Tito could carry him all day. Tito headed for the bathroom. Cooper didn't argue, but he could feel how tense Cooper's muscles were. Tito refused to back down. He carried Cooper to the shower's panel.

"Choose our settings."

Every bedroom in the house had the same shower system. They were computerized, with personalized settings. Tito wanted Cooper to be as comfortable as possible. Cooper didn't argue. He pressed a few buttons, and the shower fired to life. Tito set Cooper on his feet and held his stare while peeling off the shirt he wore. Cooper lifted his arms, letting Tito have it. He didn't stay passive. Cooper hooked his thumbs in the waistband of Tito's underwear and dragged it down Tito's hips. He was brave as hell. Tito wanted him.

Once they were nude, Tito swept Cooper into the shower. Steam surrounded them and water pelted their bodies. Tito claimed Cooper's mouth again. He stroked Cooper's tongue and bit at his lips. Tito teased Cooper's mouth while he kneaded Cooper's ass. His dick was hard, and his body ached. He had never gone this long without actual sex. Since Cooper moved in six months ago, Tito had been completely enamored. No one else would do. Cooper stroked Tito's cock. Tito had to lock his knees when they weakened. He had to get Cooper ready to get fucked because he couldn't wait anymore. Tito knew all the best settings on this shower. He pushed a few buttons before ushering Cooper to the bench. Tito watched Cooper's every reaction as he adjusted the jets, ensuring Cooper got the most pleasure from the pressurized water. Cooper's eyes widened and a smile that felt evil even to Tito pulled at his lips. It wasn't enough to get Cooper off, but it would get him close. He grabbed the shampoo and washed Cooper's hair while

Cooper panted. Next, he washed his own hair and body while Cooper clung to the edge of the bench, looking ready to pounce. Tito took his time. Then he turned his attention to washing Cooper's body. Slow. Torturous.

"Please." The hoarse plea was the sign Tito had been waiting for. He snatched Cooper from the bench and headed for bed. Wet and uncaring, Tito tossed Cooper onto the mattress. He watched Cooper pant while he rolled on a condom and lubed the outside. Cooper wasn't thinking about his scars anymore. He openly stroked his erection while waiting for Tito to fuck him. Tito doused his fingers in lube before crawling between Cooper's thighs. He kissed Cooper's stomach right above his crown, making sure his breath brushed Cooper's cock. Then he worked two fingers inside Cooper's asshole. He was ridiculously tight. Tito would likely hurt him. It was torture to go slow. He needed Cooper distracted. A bead of pre-cum dripped from Cooper's dick. Tito licked Cooper's crown, capturing the drop on his tongue.

. . .

"Oh god."

At Cooper's gasped words, Tito swallowed Cooper's cock. Cooper's hips left the bed. He squirmed beneath Tito's suction and the fingers in his ass. Tito worked a third finger inside Cooper, stretching him. He bobbed on Cooper's dick. Cooper scratched at the sheets. Tito's erection jumped and leaked. He wanted all the pleasure Cooper's tight ass promised. When he couldn't take it any longer, Tito shot forward and pushed his dick inside Cooper's ass. A loud cry tore from Cooper. Tito froze. He pressed his forehead to Cooper's chest and squeezed his eyes shut, hoping Cooper adjusted soon. Cooper's tight heat was killing him. Tito rocked lightly, testing the waters. A low moan vibrated from Cooper. Cooper adjusted his position and thrust.

"Holy shit."

Cooper's reaction had Tito nearly sighing in relief. As he thrust again, he watched Cooper's face. Cooper's expression made something in Tito's chest shift. He looked like he witnessed a miracle. His reaction filled Tito with pride. Fuck, Cooper was something special. Tito wanted to be Cooper's first and last everything. Right now, his body had demands. Aroused didn't begin to cover the fire that burned inside Tito.

He hooked Cooper's knee and thrust, falling into a steady rhythm. They held each other's stare while Tito pumped inside Cooper. Cooper's lips parted as he fought to breathe. His face flushed. Tito absorbed every detail. Pressure climbed Tito's shaft. His pace sped. Cooper moaned, openly reaching for release. Tito tugged at Cooper's cock, helping him along. When Cooper's body tensed, Tito saw stars. Cum shot from Cooper's dick and Tito aimed the load toward his mouth. It hit his bottom lip. Tito licked the salty fluid into his mouth.

"Goddamn. That was hot."

At Cooper's claim, Tito kissed him. He wanted Cooper to taste the cum on his tongue. Today was only the beginning. There was so much Tito could show him. Cooper bit Tito's bottom lip and the orgasm he had been holding at bay exploded through him. He shook as he pumped the condom full of cum. Tito already wanted more. Maybe the day wouldn't be peaceful, but Tito fully intended to keep Cooper's mind busy and his body burning. They weren't finished.

SIX

DESPITE IT ONLY BEING TWO hours away, the weather was much milder in San Diego and Tito still hadn't told him where they were going. Each time Cooper asked, Tito kept reminding him it was a surprise. Cooper was oddly nervous for no reason at all. As Tito pulled into the driveway of a large brick home, Cooper's discomfort doubled. He hadn't let Cooper book them a hotel room, and Cooper somehow doubted Tito had rented this family-style home with a football in the yard. That meant Tito knew who lived inside.

. . .

His suspicions were confirmed when a middle-aged woman rushed the driveway, jumping up and down. A man followed her at a slower pace.

"Tito. Oh my goodness. Look at you. My baby is home."

Cooper nearly groaned aloud. It was Tito's parents. Cooper could see the resemblance between the man and Tito. Tito slid from the SUV and hugged his mom. With his arm wrapped around his mom's waist, Tito circled the vehicle and opened the door for Cooper.

Tricia didn't look surprised to see Cooper. That meant this trip was planned. Cooper gave a small wave he feared looked as uncomfortable as he was. "Hi."

Tricia didn't seem the least bit put off by Cooper's open nervousness. "Hey. You must be Cooper."

. . .

Cooper nodded. "I am. You must be Mrs. De Luca."

Tito helped him from the SUV and Tricia shook his hand. "Please call me Tricia. This is my husband, Dante."

Cooper held tight to Tito's hand and gave Dante the same awkward wave.

Tito kissed his ear. "You said anywhere I wanted to go," he whispered before pulling away.

Cooper had said that.

Dante moved forward, shook Cooper's hand, and then turned his attention Tito's way. "You should take your bags to your room and then come check out your baby. I've been starting her once a week and taking her out now and then since you never visit." There was no missing the admonishment in that last bit.

. . .

"I have a busy schedule." No one listened to Tito's weak argument.

Tricia took Cooper's hand. "You come with me."

Cooper tried not to look behind him, seeking help from Tito. He might not be entirely comfortable, but he wasn't weak. Cooper had lived on the street, for fuck's sake. He could sleep in Tito's parents' house. This was nothing.

Tricia led Cooper through the living room. It was a hodgepodge of various furniture. Nothing matched, and every flat surface was covered in picture frames. Each image showed a different smiling face. Cooper fought the urge to look at each one. He wanted to see Tito in his younger days.

They headed inside the kitchen. Tricia spoke over her shoulder. "Enzo and Marco are having a cookout tonight. I have to pack the food I'm taking so we can get going." She pointed at a stool next to the kitchen island. "Keep me company. I've been dying to meet you. You're all Tito has talked about for at least six months now."

Cooper didn't sit right away. "Would you like some help?"

Tricia gave a dismissive wave. "Nah. I've got it."

Even though he felt useless, Cooper sat. The kitchen was huge and had tons of cabinets. There was a large dining room table nearby and lots of stools scattered about, as if people usually gathered in the kitchen. Cooper didn't know what to talk about with a mom, but he couldn't handle the silence.

"I didn't know Tito's family lived in San Diego until we got here. I thought he was born in L.A."

. . .

Tricia nodded while shoving Tupperware into a leather backpack. "He was. We moved here a month after Tito turned eighteen. Both of our older boys are stationed here. We wanted to be closer to them, but L.A. was in Tito's blood. He hated moving away from his friends. A week after the move, Hudson performed for the troops and Marco got a special meet and greet with Hudson as part of him receiving a special heroism award. He got to take us with him. Hudson and Tito were immediate friends. He offered Tito a job and a place to live in the town he loved, and Tito was gone quicker than I could formulate an opinion. When you have four ambitious kids, it's impossible to keep them living nearby their entire lives. It seems like at least one always gets away. At least it's a quick two-hour trip."

Cooper enjoyed hearing about Tito's life. He wanted to know everything. "Tito has a sister too, right?"

Tricia flashed him a smile. "Yes. Anna. She married one of Enzo's friends. Another Navy man. He got reassigned to the Naval Air Station in Meridian three months ago, taking my grand babies with them. It's hard having one son in L.A., two in San Diego, and now my grand babies in Mississippi." She locked on to him with a conspiratorial gaze. "I don't suppose you could lure Tito to Mississippi while I work on my oldest two."

A bark of laughter burst from Cooper. "I don't have that kind of pull."

Tricia waved off his words. "Meh. I don't guess I can ask him to give up the home he loves anyhow. I just worry sometimes that he thinks we're always choosing his siblings over him and that's why he never visits."

Cooper might not know much about how good families worked, but he knew Tito. "I don't think you have to worry about that. Tito genuinely has no time off. He's happy, though. Well-adjusted. You raised a good man." Cooper liked her for that reason alone.

. . .

She stacked a couple of six packs into another bag. "Tito tells me your parents have passed. Do you have any siblings?"

Damn. It was obvious Tito had spoken to her recently, which made sense, since he planned this visit. He wondered how much she knew. "No. It's just me. Unless you count Rocky, Jinx, and Hudson. They're as good as family to me. Otherwise, no."

Tricia shook her head. "I can't even imagine being completely alone in the world at your age. You're right, though. Hudson is a great guy. Once he considers someone family, it's for life. I've been grateful for him over the years. He's been very good to Tito."

Their conversation petered out, making Cooper wish he knew what to say. He knew she was just a person and he could probably find something to talk about. The thing was, he wanted her to like him, but he didn't think he was very likable.

. . .

Tricia finished packing the food and focused on him. She had dark hair and eyes. Tito looked nothing like her, but she had a kindness to her. Cooper tried for a small smile. He didn't doubt for a second his discomfort was written all over his face. Tricia was obviously unfazed. She wiped Cooper's mind clean. "You have no idea how thrilled Dante and I are to have you. Tito has never introduced us to anyone before. He loves you very much."

Cooper's lips parted in surprise.

Tito and Dante burst into the kitchen, taking up too much space and saving Cooper from saying anything dumb. Cooper eyed Tito's smiling face. His chest warmed. Tito's eyes were bright with happiness. Cooper didn't know if Tricia was right. It didn't matter. He loved Tito enough for the both of them. Cooper would endure a thousand uncomfortable trips to see Tito smile. Nothing mattered more. This was love.

This trip had been a risk. Tito hadn't known how Cooper would react to meeting his family. Cooper usually did well with strangers. Living in the streets had made him pretty brave and versatile. Tito recognized this was different. There was a lot of pressure in meeting the parents when dating. Not to mention, Cooper hadn't had a good experience with his own parents. That was exactly why Tito wanted Cooper to meet his. Tito's family was large and loud. They laughed and got rowdy. He knew Cooper would relax, eventually. Plus, they needed an unknown place to stay away from the press. Tito just needed to make sure Cooper had fun.

Tito pulled on a leather vest he had found in the garage and then reached for Cooper's hand. "Are you ready?"

Cooper smiled as he let Tito pull him to his feet. "Always."

Tito hoped that was true. Cooper hadn't met his brothers yet. Tito led Cooper to the garage. He grabbed a helmet. "This one should work for you." He plopped it onto Cooper's head before Cooper could protest. Tito went to work, adjusting the strap. "Have you ever been on a motorcycle?"

A myriad of emotions passed over Cooper's features, but he didn't let Tito down. "No, but lucky for you, I'm currently trying new things."

A chuckle rose and stuck in Tito's throat. Cooper was so much fun. Tito pulled on his helmet. "This way, sexy."

Tito threw his leg over his Harley and motioned for Cooper to join him. Cooper scrambled on behind him, making Tito proud. Then Cooper's arms encircled him, and his body pressed against Tito's back. Tito stroked Cooper's hand before firing the bike to life. His mom rode with his dad on their Harley. They headed out. He had this ridiculous feeling—like they were riding off into the sunset. Tito genuinely was sickeningly in love with Cooper. One of these days, he had to admit that.

.   .   .

It took them less than fifteen minutes to get to Enzo and Marco's place. The twins had always stuck together. They had been born a minute apart, held hands in every baby picture, and been inseparable throughout life. They had joined the Navy together and had never lived apart. Tito imagined one day they would die together, because they didn't know any other way.

Marco swept in the moment Tito parked and stole Cooper. "Well, hello there, sexy. You must be Cooper." That was all Tito heard before Marco towed Cooper away like he owned him. Tito wasn't too worried. Both his brothers were players. Cooper was too levelheaded for either of them. He looked absolutely tiny with Enzo and Marco hovering over him, flirting. They were both six feet and two hundred pounds of sleek muscle. They looked like the seducers they were while staring at Cooper.

"I like him."

.   .   .

Tito tore his gaze away from his lecher brothers and focused on his mom at her claim. "I'm glad to hear that."

Tricia nodded. "He's a bit serious for someone so young, but he's very polite."

Tito scowled. He didn't like her undertone. "He doesn't know how to act around parents. Give him some time."

At his chastisement, Tricia looked taken aback. "I was being serious. I really do like him. He's just very young."

Since it obviously couldn't be avoided, Tito pulled his mom aside. "Look, I wasn't planning on saying anything because it's not my business to tell. I get that Cooper is young. Everyone keeps pointing it out to me, but you don't know him. He spent two years homeless after surviving the worst abuse imaginable.

His dad basically tortured him and murdered his mother. Cooper isn't young on the inside. He's really amazing, but he likely has no clue how to act around you or Dad. Honestly, he's probably a little terrified of you two. So please give him a chance. I brought him here so he can see there are good parents out there."

Tricia had tears in her eyes. "Why didn't you say anything? I can't believe anyone hurt that sweet boy. No wonder he looked horrified to be left alone with me. It took a lot of bravery for him to talk to me for as long as he did."

"Don't say anything," Tito said, emphasizing each word. He knew his mom. She couldn't keep a secret. "I didn't ask him if it was okay to tell you."

She pretended to zip her lips. "I won't say a word. Now, let's go rescue him from your brothers. Jesus, they're pawing all over him."

. . .

Tito's head whipped around at his mom's claim. Sure enough, Enzo had Cooper's hand pressed to his lips and Marco was down on one knee, tying Cooper's shoe.

"Jesus fucking Christ." Tito muttered the words under his breath as he stomped across the backyard. His brothers couldn't be trusted to be alone with anyone at all under the sun over the age of eighteen. "Really, guys? You're thirty-one. When do you plan to settle down?"

Matching evil grins turned his way. "Never."

Cooper laughed at their simultaneous answer. He smiled up at Tito and Tito forgot his anger. "They were just giving me the dirt on you. Did they really catch you getting blown by the JV coach in the locker room your sophomore year?"

A loud groan escaped Tito. He had literally left them alone for less than ten minutes. At this rate, Cooper would dump him by the end of the night. He looked around, searching for any way out of this when he spotted his mom whispering to his dad. Fuck his life. His dad was staring at Cooper, looking outraged. Tito wondered if he should kick himself to the curb. It looked to be a long night.

Cooper startled and then pulled his phone from his pocket. He checked the face. A sexy growl escaped him. "It's Baker. He's at Quaver and wants my input on some of Dad's things."

Tito fought the urge to toss Cooper's phone into the pool. "Let him know you're out of town and will deal with it later. Fuck. I don't understand why this guy is acting like all this has to be done right this second. The estate is still paying everyone's salary. He needs to stop rushing you."

Even Tito didn't completely understand his irritation. There was just something about Baker Tito didn't trust. He was young, rich, and had obviously known Cooper long enough to know about Cooper's abuse. Yet he had done nothing. Maybe that was the gist of it. Too many people had turned a blind eye to Cooper's suffering. Tito couldn't stomach it. He didn't understand. All he could figure was money was the motivation. If anyone in Cooper's life had stood up for Cooper, then the money train would end. Tito hated everyone who had stayed quiet.

Cooper stroked Tito's stomach, bringing Tito back to the present. He realized Enzo and Marco had abandoned them and were now huddled with his parents, whispering. Tito wondered if he should apologize now or later.

There was a deep line between Cooper's eyebrows, distracting him. "Are you okay, baby?"

At Cooper's question, Tito realized Cooper was worried about him. Also, Tito was scowling and hadn't noticed. He forced his features clear and a smile to his lips. "I'm sorry, angel. I brought you here to get you away from everything and now Baker is texting you. Ignore me. It's just that I love you and all this is..." It hit Tito what he had said. He didn't know if he should keep talking like nothing happened or own it.

Cooper chose for him. "You love me?"

Tito rubbed the back of his neck. He swore the temperature rose by twenty degrees. "Yeah. I guess I should've told you in a more romantic way."

"I love you too."

Every ounce of discomfort slipped away at Cooper's admission. Tito brought Cooper's hand to his mouth and held it there while holding Cooper's stare. He hoped Cooper saw all the love in his eyes and understood how badly he wished they were alone. Tito needed Cooper to know that he would go to the ends of the earth for him.

. . .

"Okay. Enough mooning. Let someone else have a turn," Enzo said, stealing Cooper away.

Before Tito could complain, Marco threw an arm over Tito's shoulders and steered him away from the group. "I have news."

"Okay."

"Secret news," Marco said, sounding cryptic. "So you can't tell Mom."

Tito rolled his eyes. He had already made the mistake of telling his mom one secret tonight. Tito wouldn't make that mistake again any time soon. "You know me."

Marco's dark green eyes moved over Tito's face for a second before nodding, as if he had decided he could trust Tito. "Enzo and I are retiring next month."

. . .

"Seriously?" Tito hadn't meant to be so loud or excited. He just worried about his brothers.

Marco shushed him while looking around, as if ensuring they hadn't drawn any attention their way. He seemed to be satisfied they hadn't caught any curiosity. "We're not telling Mom and Dad yet, because we're moving back to L.A."

Tito hissed. He knew how much hell he caught for living a mere two hours away. No matter what his mom said to the contrary, Marco and Enzo were her favorites. She had moved to be closer to them. "Yeah. That won't go over well."

"I know." Marco sounded like he did, but Tito doubted Marco had any real clue how bad it would be. "But we're hoping Mom will use the opportunity to consider moving closer to Anna. She's really missing the boys and we're about to be crazy busy with a new business."

. . .

"A new business? That sounds promising."

Marco nodded. "We're going in with a friend of ours to open a bar in L.A., hoping to lure in service members and veterans."

"That sounds perfect for you." Tito's gaze found Cooper as he said the words. Cooper and Tricia had their heads together, looking at her phone. It seemed his mom had roped Cooper into looking at all her pictures. Cooper's smile looked genuine. It did Tito's heart good to see Cooper happy with his family. He had been a little worried about Cooper meeting everyone. They could be a little too outspoken. Tito knew the age gap thing would be an issue they would have an opinion about. The last thing Tito wanted was for Cooper to feel unwanted or attacked.

"Wow. You're really in love with this guy."

At Marco's words, Tito tore his gaze away from Cooper. He flashed his brother a smile. "Yeah. I don't know what happened, really. He showed up one day and that was it for me. I knew immediately he was the one."

Marco shook his head. A boyish smile stretched his lips. "Damn. I really want to tell you you're an idiot, since being a rock star's bodyguard comes with all the ass. But I can't. You look too happy." He was. Tito had never been so intoxicated by life. He looked forward to getting up every day and spending it with Cooper. Tito would do anything to keep him.

It was hard to keep smiling with Baker blowing up his phone. Cooper tried hiding his irritation. When he didn't have an incoming text, he was truly enjoying himself. Tito's brothers were something else. Cooper hadn't expected such huge flirts. They weren't an exact pair. Their eyes were different. Enzo reminded Cooper the most of Tito. They had the same hazel eyes, and Enzo had a sliver of Tito's calm demeanor. Marco had gorgeous dark green eyes. His every movement screamed he was a player.

Cooper didn't doubt for a second women and men dropped like flies at their feet. It was a good thing Cooper was completely in love with Tito. Otherwise, Cooper might get caught in their web.

For the twentieth time, Cooper's phone buzzed. He knew who it would be before he checked the face. Baker was a tad angry with Cooper. Since Cooper had been adamant about dumping Quaver as quickly as possible, Baker worked overtime to make it happen. It seemed his overtime meant Cooper's involvement, and Cooper didn't want the job. Baker kept peppering him with questions about his wishes when it came to various objects in the house. While Cooper understood everything was his now and all of this should be on him, he didn't know yet how to face it. When Cooper had run away, he hadn't intended to ever look back. He was overwhelmed. When Cooper had to face too much at once, he shut down. He couldn't help it. Cooper had issues.

"Why do you keep looking at your phone like it beat you up in school?"

. . .

Tito's sudden appearance and quip made Cooper's anxiety disappear. He opened his mouth to bitch about Baker and a van pulled up to the curb, followed quickly by another. Reporters began rolling in like a cloud of locusts. Cooper stared in horror. The same questions from the beach were hurled his way. What had really happened to his mother? Did the police have any leads on his father's killer? Where had Cooper been the past few years? What would he do now? At a picnic table in Marco and Enzo's backyard, Cooper couldn't move. He was paralyzed. Tricia put her arm around him. The men worked together to force the press to the curb and off private property. Then Tito was there.

"What in the fuck is going on? How do they keep finding you?"

"Language," Tricia said, fussing at Tito's outburst.

Cooper's shock hadn't ebbed. Tito's family had heard them talk about Cooper's parents. He couldn't imagine what they were thinking. They probably thought Tito should run.

Tito stooped in front of Cooper and took his hands. "Who knew you were coming here, baby?"

Cooper managed a shrug. "I don't know. I didn't even know I was coming here. You kept our destination a secret."

Even though Cooper could tell Tito was angry, Tito didn't take it out on him. Tito rubbed Cooper's hands and forearms, as if trying to comfort him. "Help me think, baby. Is there anyone who knew where we were surfing and also knows about this place?"

Cooper shook his head. "You. Hudson." The truth hit, stopping his breath. Anger slammed into him. "Baker." He rushed to explain. "The day we went surfing, he wanted me to come by his office to sign something and I told him no. I told him we already had plans to go surfing at Surfrider beach. Since his office isn't anywhere near there, I made a point of telling him Surfrider. Then, tonight, you told me to tell him I was out of town and couldn't help him with the estate. So I told him we were visiting your family in San Diego and I couldn't come by. For someone like him, it wouldn't take but half a minute to find out where your family lives in San Diego." His father only had the best of everything. That meant a shark for a lawyer too.

Tito shot to his feet. He looked angrier than Cooper had ever seen. "I'll be back." He headed for his bike.

Cooper scrambled after him. "Where are you going?"

"To have a little chat with Baker," Tito said, pulling on his helmet.

. . .

"That's a two-hour drive one way, Tito. Let it go. We can deal with it later."

Tito shook his head. "I'm not letting this guy upend your life. You've been through enough. If he's sending the press after you, he's explaining why. His answer will determine if he gets to keep his teeth."

Cooper was horrified. He didn't know what to do. His gaze shot Enzo's way, looking for backup. In the half second that he looked away, Tito fired the bike to life and left before Cooper could stop him.

Enzo moved to Cooper's side. "Do you know where he'll find this guy?"

Cooper nodded, feeling helpless.

Enzo took his hand. "Then let's go."

. . .

In a flash, the entire family were loaded up in Enzo's Yukon and they headed out. Cooper typed the address into Enzo's phone. Enzo broke the speed limit all the way there, trying to catch up to Tito. Cooper gave them the cliff notes on his life and Baker on the way. They made it in record time. As Enzo pulled into the driveway and Quaver came into view, the same feeling of being trapped and helpless overcame him he had felt all his life. It was as if the house remembered—like evil lived in the walls.

"Goddamn. This is your house?"

Cooper shook his head at Marco's question. "It's my father's house." Reality slammed into him for the first time since Baker had shown at Hudson's. "I guess it really is mine now." He didn't have time to drown in that pond of despair. Tito's bike was parked out front and the doors stood open on the house. The moment Cooper was outside the car, he heard the yelling. He raced inside to find Tito hovering over Baker inside the living room, shouting him down. Claude tried intervening.

. . .

Dante and Marco pulled Tito away before he did anything stupid. Enzo rubbed Cooper's back while Cooper stood, choking on the past. He never handled shouting well.

Baker moved his way the second Tito was out of his path. "We have to talk."

Cooper shook his head, rallying. "You sent the press after me. I don't owe you anything. How could you do it?" Now that he was here, the anger set in. Baker had known Cooper's father. He knew what Cooper's life had been like. Cooper didn't understand why he could be so cruel. "Haven't I suffered enough? Do you need more blood from me? I have nothing left to give, Baker. What could you possibly have to gain?"

"If I could just speak to you alone for half a minute, I could explain." Baker's desperation showed in every word. He looked every bit as crazed as Cooper felt.

. . .

"No. You don't get to be alone with me."

"May I speak with you in the other room?" Claude's whisper sounded like a shout through a megaphone with the tension at an all-time high. Cooper's gaze shot Claude's way. The moment he realized Claude was speaking to Tito, he turned his fury back Baker's way. Cooper had been silently seething his entire life. Now his anger had been set free. Baker looked like a damn good target.

"What could you possibly have to say to me that would excuse setting the goddamn press on me? How fucking dare you?"

Baker snapped beneath Cooper's rage. "I need someone to pressure you into telling the truth. If enough press takes interest, eventually someone will offer you enough money for you to tell your side of the story. I have to know what happened to Jessica. I need to know if he killed her because—"

.   .   .

"Yes," Cooper yelled, completely losing his temper. He was tired of people asking him about his mother's murder. "Anyone who knew my dad should know that answer. He was an evil, sadistic bastard. I'm surprised he didn't kill us both sooner. If anyone should know what he did or didn't do, it's you. You're his lawyer. Didn't you represent him?"

Baker shook his head. His rage visibly bled away. "I'm not that type of lawyer and that's not what I was going to say. I need to know if he killed her because of me."

Cooper deflated. Confusion had his temper slipping away. "Why would you even ask that?"

For a moment, Baker stared at Cooper in silence. Then he took a deep breath and spoke.

"Because we were having an affair."

· · ·

A small laugh escaped Cooper without thought. "That's ridiculous. You're like ten years younger than her." He heard himself. Cooper was almost eleven years younger than Tito. That argument shouldn't have even rated in Cooper's top ten. Baker's claim just seemed so insane.

Baker looked at Cooper as if he had lost his mind. "I'm thirty-nine. Jessica was only two years older than me."

Cooper's forehead furrowed. He didn't understand. His mom had seemed so meek. The picture Baker painted didn't match the image in his head of his mother.

Baker moved to the couch and sat. His gaze never wavered from Cooper. "Jessica was incredibly beautiful. You look just like her."

Cooper's knees nearly gave out. He moved to the loveseat across from Baker and sat. Enzo filled the space beside him and rubbed his back. Cooper fought to merge the memory of his mom with this new piece of her. "She wasn't brave enough to have an affair. I mean, she couldn't even stand up to my dad when he didn't like her clothes. By my teenage years, I don't think I even saw her, but maybe once a week. She never left her room."

"She wasn't in her room. She would lock her bedroom door and then sneak away to be with me."

The air left Cooper's lungs. She had left him to face Kristoff alone. He wished he was more surprised.

When Cooper didn't respond, Baker filled the silence. "I used to come by often with various paperwork and contracts for Kristoff. He was usually drunk and kept me waiting for hours. I spent a lot of time with your mom. We found we had a lot in common and we just..." Baker cleared his throat, as if uncomfortable talking about his personal life in front of a room full of strangers, but he pushed on.

"Kristoff walked in on us embracing and he tossed me out. The next day, she was gone. I need to know if it's because of me. Did I get her killed?"

Cooper made a helpless gesture. Too much had happened. His brain was in overload. This man looked genuinely broken, as if he had truly loved Cooper's mom. Cooper tried to force his memories of that day to the forefront of his mind after years of trying to bury them. For him, family was the ultimate F word, and he needed to see this through so he could leave them behind once and for all.

"I genuinely don't know what happened that night. They put me on a plane to New York that morning, and the police were at my room the next day. I don't know why he did it. Maybe it had always only been a matter of time. I'm just as lost as you are."

"That's because he didn't do it."

.   .   .

Cooper's head whipped around. Claude stood in the doorway with Tito. Tito helped Claude into the nearest chair. Claude looked twenty years older today. He met Cooper's stare. "I'm so sorry, Coop. I know I should've told you what happened before today, but there are some conversations you don't know how to start, and I didn't want to risk reaching out to you."

"What are you talking about? According to the police, there was no one else here that night. Even Mary and you weren't here that weekend. If not Dad, then who?"

"She killed herself."

Cooper blinked. That was the craziest thing he had ever heard. He couldn't help but say as much. "You're telling me she stabbed herself to death. That's insane."

. . .

"Is it?" Claude sounded tired. "Maybe so. At the time, it seemed a completely rational reaction to the total helplessness of the situation. Your father was as powerful as he was cruel. He was a very rich man who played golf with judges on the weekend. No one knew how to save you or her. There was no one to call outside your father's reach. We were all powerless. Your mother, most especially. You were her baby and there was nothing she could do. So she plotted and waited until there was no chance suspicion would fall on you. She sent Mary and me to the beach house a few days beforehand under the guise of getting it ready for the family. Then she made him angry. She let him drink and beat her until he passed out, then I helped her set things up so it would look like he was the one who stabbed her. Afterward, I returned to the beach house. God forgive us, we didn't know what else to do."

Cooper sat in stunned silence. Nothing made sense.

"That explains the judge's sealed decision to drop the charges against Kristoff. The investigators must've learned the truth and Kristoff must have paid off the judge to keep the matter sealed."

Claude nodded at Baker's words. "Kristoff kept me on because he was sadistic and blackmailed me into staying. I faced no charges as long as I remained silent and in his employ. Kristoff cared more about his reputation than anything in the world. He'd much rather look like a murderer than the woman and child beating bastard he was." Baker met Cooper's gaze. "He'd much rather let his son live in the street than admit to any wrongdoing in the public eye." He held Cooper's stare, looking like a beaten down old man. "I understand if you need to hate me for my part, but please forgive your mother. She didn't feel like there was any other way to escape."

Cooper looked around the room at all the people who were getting an ugly inside glimpse at his life, and a wave of sadness washed over him. There was no way Tito's family would want him to be a part of them now. They would warn Tito against getting mixed up with someone this fucked up. No one understood how badly he wanted to be free of this legacy. He didn't want to be Cooper Whitaker anymore. Cooper didn't want to be responsible for his mother's death. He didn't want any of this. Cooper couldn't take any more bullshit from life.

He met Baker's stare. "My dad killed my mom. It doesn't matter if he wasn't the one who stabbed her, and it equally matters not at all about your affair. Living under the thumb of Kristoff Whitaker killed her long before she stabbed herself. I should know." Cooper's voice broke as he pressed his hand to his chest. He had to stiffen his spine and clear his throat to continue. "He killed me too." Cooper stood. "If anything else needs to be signed or decided, please send it through your partner. I don't want to see you again. If the press hounds me anymore because of you, I promise I will make you sorry. I don't care about you, the affair, or anything else for that matter. I died in this house too. My body is just too stubborn to give up." Cooper didn't meet anyone's gaze as he walked away. Tito followed him outside. He tried talking to Cooper, but Cooper didn't hear a word. It had only been a matter of time before the crack in his soul shattered him. Cooper had always wondered what would finally shove him over the edge. It turned out that it was knowing too much that did him in.

All of his life, Cooper had believed his mom was simply too weak to save him. The truth was... he didn't know anymore. There was a part of him that felt like if she was strong enough to risk having an affair, then she could have done anything, including saving him. On the other hand, maybe Claude was right. There was no escaping Kristoff, and Baker had been the only freedom she had ever known.

Tito was still talking.

Cooper looked his way. "Will you take me home, please?"

Tito's expression fell, but he headed for his bike. Cooper climbed on behind him and didn't look back. It didn't matter whose feelings he hurt. He couldn't feel a thing anyhow. At Hudson's, there wasn't any press waiting. They easily made it inside the house.

Tito kept trying to talk to Cooper all the way to Cooper's room. Still, no sound penetrated the haze coating his brain.

At his bedroom door, Cooper finally managed to meet Tito's stare.

"I just want to be alone." Even Cooper heard how dead his voice sounded.

Tito looked ready to shake Cooper, but he gave Cooper a sharp nod instead. "Okay. I have to head back to my parents' place and exchange the bike for the SUV. I'll grab our luggage and head back. If you need anything before I get home, call me or get Brent, okay?"

Cooper nodded. He didn't understand why he couldn't feel.

Tito eyed him. "I love you."

.   .   .

"I love you too." It was just words. Cooper felt nothing. There was a chill in his chest where his heart should be. Tito brushed a kiss across his lips and left him alone. Cooper's teeth chattered, forcing him to lock his jaw. The past pounded at his brain in a way it hadn't in years. His father's voice echoed in his head, telling Cooper he was useless and worthless. His existence did nothing but ruin others. According to his father, Cooper had cost his mother her looks. Now, according to Claude, Cooper had cost his mother her life. It should have been him. Maybe if he had succumbed to the abuse, his mom wouldn't have. She might have gained the strength to leave and have a good life with Baker.

Cooper locked his bedroom door. His gaze skimmed the room. How long would it take before his neediness sucked the life from Tito? Hudson? Rocky? Maybe he would absorb every ounce of love and light from this home, leaving it devoid of happiness. Cooper couldn't do it. He was already dead. No one else needed to suffer.

.   .   .

Cooper found his passport. His wallet and phone were already in his pocket. He wouldn't take anything else. Cooper had already taken too much from this world. He headed for the balcony. Once he swung over the edge, it wasn't that long of drop. He easily landed in the grass below.

Hudson had a large property. Cooper headed toward the woods behind the house. He didn't want to risk being seen by the guards working the front gate. It was dark, but the moon lit the way. Cooper didn't worry about getting lost. He didn't have a destination. His only plan was to save the people he loved from him. They didn't know how broken he was or how tired. When his knees gave out, Cooper curled into a ball on the ground, uncaring of the cold soil or the grass staining his clothes. Once the first tear fell, it was like a flood gate opened. Cooper was afraid of himself. He was scared of how ugly his thoughts could be. Time slipped away. The tears refused to stop. There was too much bad inside of him with nowhere to go. He had tried to live a quiet life, hoping the peace would heal him. It hadn't worked. His shattered soul was glass shards, cutting away at his insides while trying to escape him. He was like one of those severely abused wild animals that couldn't be helped. Cooper needed someone to put him down because it was the kind thing to do. He didn't know how to be normal. Life was too overwhelming. It was never quiet, no matter where he went. He hoped there was peace in death.

SEVEN

RAGE AND HURT pumped through Tito's veins. He was more thankful than he could articulate that his parents hadn't made it home yet. He traded the bike for the SUV and grabbed their luggage in peace. Tito wasn't ready to talk to anyone. Even in death, Cooper's parents were trying to break him. Tito refused to let it happen. Cooper belonged to him now. No one hurt him. Not even ghosts of the past. Then there was the whole thing with Cooper saying he was already dead. Tito couldn't take it. He needed to help Cooper.

By the time he made it home, his temper had cooled a hair. Then he realized Cooper was gone. Tito wasn't the least bit surprised Cooper had run away. In fact, he had subconsciously been braced and prepared for it for a while. He tracked the GPS on Cooper's phone for two miles until he found him asleep in the woods. He looked a complete mess. It was obvious he had been crying. Dirt streaked his face. When Tito lifted Cooper into his arms, Cooper's body stayed limp—like there wasn't any life left in him. Tito might have panicked if Cooper hadn't immediately buried his face against Tito's chest, openly seeking warmth. Still, Tito hurt for his angel. In some ways, Cooper was like a severely abused animal. Tito was the only person Cooper fully trusted not to hurt him. It was as humbling as it was heartbreaking. Tito had to keep his baby safe.

At the house, he carried Cooper to his room. After settling Cooper on the bed, Tito stripped away Cooper's dirty clothes. Cooper didn't help or make a sound. He was a rag doll, accepting his fate. Once Tito had Cooper stripped out of his dirty clothes, he risked leaving him alone long enough to get a washcloth. When he returned, Cooper hadn't moved at all. His eyes were open, but he stared at nothing— like he was dead. Just as he claimed. As Tito cleaned

Cooper's face, Cooper began to shake. His teeth chattered from the power of it, and it hit Tito that Cooper was in shock. He quickly tossed the washcloth aside, stripped, and climbed into bed next to Cooper. Tito piled the covers on top of them and held Cooper as tightly as he could, sharing his warmth. For a moment, Cooper still didn't react. Finally, he blinked, as if coming back to reality.

Cooper looked broken as he met Tito's gaze. "Why did she have to kill herself for me? I can't live with that."

Tito brushed his fingers through Cooper's hair. "I don't think she did it for you." Some pain left Cooper's expression. Tito kept going. "I mean, if you think about it, she could've just stabbed your dad in his sleep and really saved you. Instead, she chose to set him up. To me, it doesn't sound like she thought of you at all. She only used you as an excuse to make him pay. She wanted him to suffer. Your mom knew nothing mattered to Kristoff as much as his reputation. She wanted to ruin him, not rid the world of him. It had nothing to do with you."

. . .

Cooper blinked. His gaze seemed unfocused, as if he had turned inward. He blinked again and his gaze focused on Tito. "You're right. It wasn't about me. I couldn't think. Nothing Baker or Claude said fit. I lived in that house. My whole life, I've been hyper aware that she did nothing to help me. She didn't do it for me. It's strange that I feel better now."

"I disagree," Tito said, settling onto his side and holding Cooper's stare. "You're just the most sensible person I know, and people were saying one thing, and—in your heart—you knew it wasn't true. Nothing that happened in that house was ever about you. Obviously, you still suffered, but none of it was ever deserved or because you're lacking in some way. You were surrounded by monsters. It was always about their sickness. But you really are free now, baby. You can leave it behind and I'll be here with you. Just let me know what you want to do. If you want to start counseling, I'll take you. If you want to move to a new country, change your name, surf all day, and eat coconuts to survive, I'll do that with you too." A lump rose in Tito's throat. "Just please don't run away from me again."

Cooper visibly swallowed, as if witnessing Tito's pain physically hurt him. He stroked Tito's cheek. "I won't, but I wasn't running away from you. I was trying to outrun me."

"Why?"

Cooper shrugged.

Tito didn't back down. Cooper needed to be honest with him. "It's okay, baby. You can tell me anything."

When Cooper responded, he sounded almost ashamed of his confession. "My dad was evil, genuinely. What if I am too?"

. . .

It took everything Tito had not to smile. He would never laugh at Cooper's fear. It was just a bit funny to him, picturing Cooper being mean to anyone. "You're not. There isn't a drop of cruelty in you."

Cooper didn't respond right away. When he did, he sounded stronger. "I can be mean. I told Baker not to contact me again, even though I know he only did what he did because he's hurting."

This time, Tito couldn't fight his smile. "Baby, that's not being mean. That's setting a boundary."

"I've also chosen not to forgive my mom yet."

That made sense to Tito. "You're completely entitled to that."

Cooper regained a little more color and life by the second. "I'm also enraged our trip was ruined, and that everyone thinks I'm too young for you. Maybe one day you'll start to believe it too and break my heart."

"Nothing you're describing makes you a bad person," Tito said, trying to reassure Cooper. "You wanted to do something nice for me because you're amazing. Evil people don't care about other people's feelings. You're afraid to get your heart broken. That's a completely normal fear. I'm scared as hell you'll wake up one day feeling like you haven't had a chance to live and leave me. You're incredible. I've never met anyone as amazing as you. You're sweet, intelligent, and gorgeous. There's nothing you're not willing to try, even when it's obvious you're scared. That's sexy as hell. If I said I wanted to go skydiving right now, you'd go."

"I don't know about that," Cooper said with a laugh. Then his expression turned serious. "Fuck, you're right. If you were serious and wanted to go, I would. That's not because I'm brave or anything, though. I'd go because I love you. There's nowhere else I'd rather be than with you, even if that means we're jumping from a plane together."

.   .   .

"I never want to lose you," Tito whispered, giving voice to his biggest fear.

Cooper's gaze moved over Tito's features. The night's drama no longer tinted Cooper's eyes. "You can't. Even when I left here earlier in a haze of anger, hurt, and confusion, I knew—in the back of mind— you would find me. Since the moment I came to live here, you've watched over me. You've kept me safe from everything, including myself. It's like you're my personal guardian angel. Only a complete dumbass would let you get away. It's possible I'm a little crazy. The jury is still out on that, but I'm not stupid. You're smart and fun. The well of patience you possess is insanely deep. You're sexy as hell. Most of all, I'm my best me when I'm with you. I never want to lose this connection we have. My guess is we'll never find what we have anywhere else. I think I've loved you since the first time we met."

Cooper's confession struck a chord. Tito rushed to say something he never thought he would admit. "It's crazy you said that. The first time we met, I had this overwhelming feeling we'd met before, even though I knew we hadn't. Then you moved in and there wasn't a slow build. It wasn't like I woke up one day and realized I was in love with you. It was like I've always known."

Cooper nodded along as if every word Tito spoke matched the way he felt. "Don't laugh at me, okay?"

Before Tito could ask a single question, Cooper flattened his palm against Tito's chest and pushed. Tito followed Cooper's lead, rolling onto his back. The moment he did, Cooper straddled his body.

Cooper stared down at Tito, looking vulnerable. "I don't know what I'm doing, but I want to be in control."

Goddamn. That was hot. Cooper's actions were also exactly what Tito had been trying to explain earlier. He didn't realize it, but Cooper was one hundred times braver than anyone Tito had ever met. Most people never exposed their hearts the way Cooper did. He was badass. There was a fire inside Cooper no one could extinguish. Tito wanted to touch it.

Cooper kissed him. The way his tongue lightly brushed Tito's was a sweet seeking. In a flash, everything changed. The temperature in the room shot up by ten degrees. Tito couldn't focus on anything other than the way Cooper's tongue moved against his, twisting and exploring. Even though Tito was harder than steel, he would have been fine to do nothing more than kiss the man he loved. Being with Cooper was enough for him.

Then Cooper kissed Tito's jaw before moving to his throat. Cooper kept moving lower. By the time Cooper made it to Tito's stomach, there was little doubt about where he was headed. Every breath Tito took was labored. His muscles were so tense, Tito worried they might snap. He couldn't explain why he felt like he had never gotten a blow job before. It was Cooper. Everything they did was special.

· · ·

When Cooper's tongue lightly flicked Tito's dick, Tito nearly came. A surge of pleasure hit him like a shot of electricity. He sucked in a sharp gasp. Then Cooper's lips closed around Tito's crown. Cooper's name slipped from Tito's lips. The way Cooper lightly licked him felt innocent and questioning—like he wasn't sure he did anything right. Tito thought he would lose his mind. He fought not to immediately blow. Tito had never been more hyper focused.

Cooper never sucked more than the tip of Tito's cock, but then he lightly squeezed Tito's balls. Tito grabbed the headboard to stop himself from forcing Cooper's head down to take him deeper. He was half insane with need. Tito wanted to pin Cooper beneath him and fuck him hard. He also wanted to stay put and let Cooper torture him all night.

Tito stared down the line of his body, watching everything. Light green eyes met his stare. Tito's muscles jerked. Cooper was beautiful. Tito would love him for the rest of his life, no matter what. He knew it then. Cooper could dump him, move on, and never speak to Tito again. Tito would still be right here, silently loving Cooper. There was no one else out there who could replace Cooper for him.

"You should marry me."

"Okay," Cooper said before going right back to his task, as if nothing happened.

Tito blinked. He wasn't sure what just happened. His proposal had been one hundred percent serious. He wasn't sure if Cooper had taken it that way or if Cooper's reply had been a yes. Damn. No one fucked with him or confused him like Cooper. He couldn't take it.

"For the record, we're engaged now."

Cooper stopped and met Tito's stare. "Okay. Am I boring you? I'm sorry I don't know what I'm doing."

. . .

A smile exploded across Tito's face. "Damn, baby. You just pulled a marriage proposal from me. I don't think you should apologize for any lack of skill. No one else has ever made me want them forever."

Cooper blushed.

Tito couldn't take it. "Let's do this." He sat up and coaxed Cooper into turning around so he could sit on Tito's face while sucking Tito's cock. "That's better," Tito said before swallowing Cooper's dick.

"Oh my god."

Pride swelled in Tito's chest at Cooper's gasped words. He adored pleasuring his angel. When Cooper's hot mouth sucked Tito's cock again, Tito's hips left the bed. He let Cooper fuck his mouth while his mind stayed locked on the light suction on his dick. Tito kneaded Cooper's ass cheeks, trying to cling to sanity. His muscles tensed. He held his breath. His balls drew up tight. Cooper unexpectedly fingered Tito's asshole. Tito blew. His entire body shook. He mindlessly went wild on Cooper's cock, sucking and swallowing. Tito held Cooper's hips in place so he couldn't get away. Cries filled the room and cum filled his mouth. Tito swallowed, oblivious to anything other than the ecstasy. His entire body shook with pleasure. Nothing existed for him any longer other than Cooper. Heaven had moved into his life when Cooper had come to live with him. Everything was perfect.

Cooper loved watching Tito sleep. Everything about Tito was hard. His body and his expression. He always looked ready to fight. Cooper knew his resting scary face was one of the many reasons he was such a good bodyguard. He looked intimidating —like he would snap a person in two and keep moving. When he slept, Tito's features didn't relax. He looked every bit as frightening. Cooper felt safe with him—like he could sleep without fear. Tito was on duty, guarding him even as he slept. No one knew how much that meant to Cooper.

. . .

Cooper didn't revisit his childhood often. He had packed those days away when he left Quaver. But some fears never left, and being pulled from a sound sleep for a round of torture was one of those memories he couldn't shake. With Tito beside him, Cooper slept like the dead without a single worry. After Tito had blown his mind, Cooper had fallen into a coma for a solid ten hours. Now that he was awake, he couldn't stop watching Tito sleep. The urge to trace Tito's features and snuggle even closer ended up driving Cooper from the bed. Tito was more put upon than any man alive because he loved Cooper. Cooper couldn't let himself disturb Tito when he finally got to rest. He slipped from the bed and across the hall to his room without waking Tito. Cooper took a quick shower before finding a baggy shirt and shorts to wear. He felt like being lazy and comfortable. Maybe he would sneak back into bed with Tito after he found some food. Cooper was starving.

After dressing, Cooper slipped downstairs, moving quickly and quietly out of pure habit. He had spent his whole life trying to move around unseen. Some habits died harder than others. To his surprise,

Tricia, Dante, and Marco were asleep on the living room floor. Rocky and Jinx were passed out on the couch. He found Enzo in the kitchen, drinking coffee and looking like death.

Cooper glanced behind him at the pile of bodies in the other room and then back at Enzo. "What did I miss last night?"

"A whole lot of alcohol," Enzo said, sounding like he had recently swallowed glass. "How are you this morning?"

Cooper shrugged. He didn't know how to answer. On one hand, he was fine. On the other, saying that sounded fucked up, all things considered.

Enzo accepted his shrug. "Would you like some coffee?"

. . .

Cooper curled his nose and headed for the fridge. "Thank you, but no thanks. I'm good with juice. Would you like some breakfast? I could make you some eggs."

Enzo winced. "No. Thank you." He looked like he fought the urge to heave at the thought of food.

Cooper hid a smile and poured himself some orange juice. As he grabbed a bowl and chose a cereal, Baker padded into the kitchen. Cooper froze. Baker looked like hell. He had a black eye and his hair stood in every direction. His clothes were more wrinkled than not.

Enzo looked between them and then slinked away, as if hoping no one noticed his abandonment.

Cooper took a slow breath, released it, and then poured his cereal. "You look like hell. What happened to your eye?"

. . .

"Tricia has one hell of a right hook."

Cooper's gaze slid back Baker's way in his shock. "Seriously?"

Baker nodded as he poured himself some coffee. "She didn't take kindly to me mistreating one of her babies, as she put it. I am to apologize today, or she'll make my other eye match. Of course, I intended to apologize anyhow."

Cooper was confused as hell, but that was pretty normal for him. "Tito is still sleeping. I don't know when he'll be up, but I'm also not sure he wants to hear your apology."

For a moment, Baker stared at him like he had grown a second head before clarifying. "Not Tito. I'm talking about you."

. . .

"Oh." Tricia had punched Baker for hurting him. Cooper didn't condone violence, but that was oddly sweet.

"I am truly sorry for all that I've done. My office has an amazing media relations department. I'll ensure you're left in peace from now on."

Cooper nodded and sipped his juice. He had said all he needed to say last night. Cooper just wanted to move on.

Hudson appeared in the kitchen. He didn't as much as blink at Baker's presence or appearance, which meant he had known Baker was there. He kissed Cooper's cheek and then stole his juice.

"I was thinking while everyone else was partying last night. Over my career, I released over one hundred and thirty songs. It's hard to narrow it down to around ten for our album, but I tried. I left a list for you to go over in the studio when you have time. It's like twenty right now, but I figured we could whittle it down together." Hudson polished off Cooper's juice. "Right now, I'm taking my men to bed." He kissed Cooper's cheek again. "Goodnight, sweetie."

"Goodnight," Cooper said, even though it was almost noon.

Hudson disappeared and Cooper found Baker staring at him. Baker didn't make him guess his thoughts. "You've really reinvented yourself here, haven't you?"

"I suppose I have," Cooper said as he fixed himself more orange juice. "When I ran away, I told everyone I met my parents had kicked me out because I'm gay. I created a whole new past for myself. It was still ugly, but nowhere near as bad as the truth." Cooper took a drink. He didn't meet Baker's stare. "It was a past I could live with. One I could survive." It hit Cooper. Baker had been desperate for the same peace. He had needed a story about Jessica's death he could live with. Thinking he had been the reason she died had been slowly driving Baker crazy. He only wanted the same peace Cooper had found in a false past. That didn't excuse what he had done, but Cooper understood now. Life wasn't black and white. Everyone was doing their best to survive the gray.

Baker set his cup aside. "I suppose I should head home. Tito wouldn't likely approve of me being here. I imagine his right hook is much worse than his mother's."

A laugh burst from Cooper without thought. He wanted to hate Baker, but he couldn't. Cooper was too mentally tired to waste a breath on hating anyone. He had to let the past go. Cooper held Baker's gaze and gave him a short nod.

A small smile touched Baker's lips. "Good luck on your new life. You deserve it." Without saying goodbye, Baker walked away. Cooper ate his cereal while standing at the counter. Pretty soon, he would crawl back into bed with Tito. Life would go on. A smile pulled at the corners of Cooper's mouth. Soon he would be Cooper De Luca, the homeless teen turned happy husband. It was a story he could live with. One with a happy ending. Nothing else mattered anymore.

EIGHT

SOOTHING waves rolled beneath Enzo's board. The sun warmed his face. Water dripped from his hair, rolling down his cheek. It had finally gotten long enough since leaving the Navy to become bothersome. On a nearby tandem board, Tito and Cooper sat facing each other. They smiled and talked, but they were too far away for Enzo to hear their conversation. He imagined it was all I love yous and other things that weren't his business. He tried not to stare. Enzo couldn't help it. It was nice to see his brother happy.

Tito had always been the serious one. Growing up, Tito had stuck by their grandmother's side, while

Marco and Enzo were always on the go, mischief-making usually. Anna had trailed behind them, trying to join in. Tito was the one who never tried to fit in. It hadn't surprised Enzo in the least when Tito had disappeared into a life the family couldn't follow. Tito was like that. He was deep waters. Tito was a lot like Hudson. That was why they had clicked so hard from their first meeting. It was like two souls who felt too much recognized a kindred spirit. Now Tito had a husband to pour all those intense and quiet emotions into. Enzo was oddly sad to be left behind. He never dreamed his little brother would marry before him. Then again, Enzo hadn't imagined any of the De Luca boys settling down. Tito might be the quiet one, but he had still lived a wild life since going to work for Hudson. Enzo hadn't expected Tito to give up the ride. Cooper was special, though. He had something Tito couldn't resist. Cooper needed Tito's loving protection. Tito had to have that in his life. He was a guardian all the way to his soul. Tito needed someone to love and keep safe. They were the perfect pair.

As Enzo looked on, Tito snagged Cooper's jaw and towed him forward, capturing his lips. Again, Enzo tried looking away. He couldn't. Enzo felt... empty. He had thought moving back to L.A. and opening a bar would fulfill something inside him. Something that had been missing from him for a while. So far, nothing had changed. It would, though. Enzo was determined to find what Tito had. It was well past the time he should have settled down. He would find his unicorn.

Tito couldn't stop kissing Cooper. His husband's lips were too delicious. He also couldn't get enough of calling Cooper his husband. Tito had never been happier. Cooper had made a lot of big and small decisions over the past few months. After signing Quaver over to Claude and Mary, he had donated half his inheritance to a charity that helped victims of child abuse. Then he had asked for help. Tito had never been prouder of anyone in his life. Cooper was the strongest person he knew.

Two months after starting counseling, Cooper had publicly announced their engagement before asking Hudson if it was okay if nothing changed. He didn't want to live away from the sheltered life he had found at Hudson's. Despite his new fortune and their marriage, Cooper needed the security of the family Hudson had given him. Cooper took Tito's last name, and nothing had changed. Tito loved that about Cooper. They had a good life. A steady one. Hudson also did better while surrounded by a supportive, chosen family. It was a win all around.

Since Cooper didn't have many things to spend his money on, he had rented the same beach house in Ibiza as Hudson had for his honeymoon. It had taken some doing with everyone's crazy schedules, but with Cooper footing the bill, he had convinced everyone to join them. Even Anna and her kids had made the trip to spend a week in Ibiza with them. It was a crazy, hot mess of a honeymoon, but Tito wouldn't have had it any other way. They were on their last week of the month-long booking. Only Enzo and Hudson's bunch remained. Everyone else had come in for a week or two, depending on their work schedules, and had headed back home. Half of Tito was ready to get back to his bed too, but he also never wanted the honeymoon to end.

· · ·

Tito kissed his way to Cooper's ear. "Hey, sexy. What are you doing for the rest of your life?"

A sexy and turned-on sounding chuckle escaped Cooper. "I'd hope to spend it with you."

Tito hummed against the shell of Cooper's ear. He was painfully aroused, and they weren't alone. "I say we head back to shore, take a shower, and then get dirty again."

"I like this plan." There was no missing the breathless note to Cooper's voice. If he ever tired of Tito constantly pawing at him, he didn't show it. His tone sounded like he was onboard with every second of nonstop affection. "But," Cooper said, running his hand down Tito's chest and heading lower. "I also kind of wonder if I can make you come in your wetsuit."

A hum rose in Tito's throat. He kind of wanted to see that too.

. . .

"Okay, guys. People can see you. By people, I mean me."

Tito laughed at his brother's discomfort. He knew it was partially faked. It took a lot to make Enzo uncomfortable, and he loved Cooper. Since the night at Quaver, where Tito's entire family had gotten a close look at the ugliness of Cooper's past, all of Tito's family had taken Cooper underneath their protective wing. No one as much as Enzo. It was like it was personal and Tito hadn't figured that one out yet.

Cooper pretended to paddle Enzo's way while blowing kisses. "Are you feeling left out? We won't let that happen."

A splash of water hit them in the face. Enzo laughed at getting his revenge but relented on guilting them. "All right. Point made. It's your honeymoon. I guess I'll just sulk alone."

. . .

Cooper's smile turned genuine. "You're never alone. You have us."

Tito couldn't tear his gaze away from Cooper. Cooper should have turned out so differently. He should be closed and keeping his heart on lockdown for fear of being shunned and hurt. Cooper was incapable of being that person. Despite everything that happened to him in his life, Cooper still took everyone into his heart like he couldn't get hurt. He was amazing. Tito's gaze moved his brother's way. They exchanged a knowing glance, as if Enzo had the same thoughts. Tito would be worthy of the man he had been blessed with. For the rest of his days, Cooper would only know happiness and warmth. That was Tito's vow. Cooper belonged to him now. Tito wouldn't let him regret it.

Keep an eye out for the next Candied Crush, *Beautifully Played*.

. . .

Please consider leaving a review at the retailer where you purchased this book. Reviews really help with a book's visibility, which allows me to continue writing more stories. Thank you, Charity.

ABOUT THE AUTHOR

Charity Parkerson is an award-winning and multi-published author with several companies. Born with no filter from her brain to her mouth, she decided to take this odd quirk and insert it in her characters.

*Eight-time Readers' Favorite Award Winner
   *2015 Passionate Plume Award Finalist
   *2013 Reviewers' Choice Award Winner
   *2012 ARRA Finalist for Favorite Paranormal Romance
   *Five-time winner of The Mistress of the Darkpath

Connect with her online:

—Sign up for my newsletter: https://sendfox.com/charityparkerson
   —Join my readers' group on Facebook: http://bit.ly/CharitysTribe
   —Website: charityparkerson.com

—Facebook:
facebook.com/authorCharityParkerson
facebook.com/TheMenofSin
—Twitter: twitter.com/CharityParkerso
—Instagram: Instagram.com/sinnerauthor
—Bookbub: https://www.bookbub.com/authors/
charity-parkerson
—Amazon page: author.to/CharityParkerson
—TikTok: http://www.tiktok.
com/@charityparkerson